THE MADDY SAGA

BOOK SEVEN

PONYGIRL GAMBIT

BY

PAUL BLADES

Cover Art by Agnes Knox
agnes.knox@gmail.com

Dark Visions Publications
darkvisionspub@gmail.com

Previously published:

Watch for publication of the other books in the Maddy Saga:

Other books by Paul Blades:

Klitzman's Isle
Klitzman's Empire
Klitzman's Paradise
Klitzman's Pawn Part One
Klitzman's Pawn Part Two
Slaver's Dozen- A Tale of Klitzman's Isle
The Taking of Cheryl Part One
The Taking of Cheryl Part Two: Slaver's Bait
Comfort Girl No. 4
Sacrifice to the Emerald God
The Blue Cantina: Anna's Surrender
The Warlord's Concubine, Books 1, 2 and 3
Dreams and Desires, Books 1 and 2

CHAPTER ONE
DRABIK'S CHOICE

Anton Drabik had a dilemma. But it was a good kind of a dilemma, the kind anyone might like to have. That is, there was really no bad choice, a kind of win/win situation. But it was going to be a tough decision, nonetheless.

Three, trembling, rabidly frightened, pretty young women were kneeling on the edge of a loading dock in a large warehouse located just outside of St. Petersburg. When they were not casting pitiable sidelong glances at him, they were staring down into the well of the dock at the three lifeless men who were lying there with Drabik's bullets lodged in their brains.

It had been a clean sweep. Stupidly, the men had posted only one inattentive, lazy guard outside the building. His lifeless body was lying in the alley with a deep, fatal laceration along his neck. The door to the warehouse wasn't even locked. It was a simple matter to creep silently inside and get the drop on the merrymakers.

The former Red Army colonel was on a mission. The warehouse belonged to one of Grobgy's crews. Axmail Grobgy, that is. In actuality, Grobgy, a fierce, powerful crime lord and a former KGB apparatchik, was Drabik's boss. He wouldn't like what had happened here at all. Drabik wasn't concerned about that. He needed the cash and that was that.

The tall, lean, scar faced killer and ponygirl trainer had decided to make his move. Too long he had chafed under the rule of the former KGB sergeant. It was the thing with

Lightning, Grobgy's prize ponygirl, that had done it, been the last straw. And so, Drabik had put his plan in motion.

It wasn't that Drabik was in love with the ponygirl. People didn't fall in love with ponygirls. They weren't human, after all. It was more like an obsession. He had trained the newly dehumanized female many months ago. It had, at the time, been nothing special. He had trained a few dozen former human females in his time. They had meant nothing to him, and if they cried and wailed while they pranced naked around the training ring, their pretty breasts flailing, a whip at their backs, well, that was just par for the course. No one expected them to like it. And it wasn't that Lightning had an especially luscious body or performed her sexual tricks more delightfully than any of the others, although she was not deficient in either respect. Most ponygirls became highly skilled sexual creatures as a direct result of their training.

In fact, when he looked at it logically, Drabik had no reason to be driven into virtual madness by the thought of losing the ponygirl forever. She was just another faceless, voiceless beast whose body was that of a human female, but whose rights to any humane treatment had been taken away.

But logic had proven useless to the cruel, conscienceless killer. His desire for the pony was so overwhelming that he could think of nothing else. And Grobgy was planning to put her in a claiming race with that fucking American billionaire, Michael Burnham. If Lightening lost the race, she would become the American's property. What would he do then? Well, he had something up his sleeve, but in order to pull it off, he needed to be sitting at the head of one of the criminal families. And that meant that Grobgy had to go, as soon as possible.

Drabik gazed at the three kneeling, terrorized young women as he pondered his choice. His sleek, black Mercedes was outside and he would pull it into the warehouse in a few minutes so that he could put the large suitcase filled with cash and the dope he had recovered into the trunk. But here was the problem. With the dope and the money in the car trunk, he doubted that he would be able to fit more than two of the three young, delectable women into it. The other would have to join their boyfriends down in the well of the loading platform. But which one?

The girls had been partying with four of Grobgy's men when Drabik entered the building. They had the radio on and the large, rundown building was filled with the screech and twang of tinny, garbled rock music. It had covered the sounds of Drabik's entrance easily. They had been gathered around a long, scratched up, wooden table when he came in. There were bottles of vodka and open boxes of Pizza Hut pizza on it. When Drabik saw the food from the American franchise, he was confirmed in his opinion that the men had to die. He was sick of the Americanization of the new Russian Republic. Everywhere he went it was McDonald's, Fedex, Pizza Hut, Britney Spears. There was no clearer sign that the stupid Communists had lost the Cold War.

Drabik had been a soldier in their army, a fierce, loyal, ruthless one. He had fought in Afghanistan, watched the debacle there unfold. The fiasco had taken down the entire system. Well, if the system could not fund one little war right on its border, maybe it deserved to, as Marx had put it, be cast into the dustbin of history. But the virtual dismemberment of the Red Army that followed had left

Drabik high and dry. It was either take a job as a peon in one of the new "enterprises", mostly foreign owned, or do what he did best.

He had started out as a bodyguard for a drug dealer and loan shark in Moscow. The money was good and the easy money and drugs attracted plenty of pussy. As pointed out by the icon of socialist theory, capitalism tends towards monopoly, and his boss was soon "taken over" by Grobgy's outfit. In a little more than a year, Drabik was taking assignments directly from the Russian mafia leader and soon became his "go to guy". When Grobgy acquired his estate in Kalikastan and began to dabble in the revived ancient sport of ponygirl racing, Drabik was a natural to follow him there.

Drabik remembered well the early days of the sport. The Russian mobs had moved into the newly independent Republic of Kalikastan, a small, fragile nation nestled in the crux of the borders of Russia and the Ukraine. There was some local opposition which was either brushed aside or otherwise dealt with and then the lunatics began to run the asylum. Neither of the newly minted governments of the other two large former Soviet republics was in a position to do anything about it since the corruption in those countries ran so high that anyone who was in a position to make a move on the gangsters was already in their pockets. Kalikastan became a convenient thoroughfare for all kinds of illicit goods. Any kind of shady transaction that needed to be hidden from the eyes of Western financial regulators could take place there.

There is some dispute as to how the ancient sport of ponygirl racing was reborn. Some say that it never really died, that all through the Czarist and Soviet eras, deep in the Kalikastani hinterland, purloined women, female political prisoners, and even, it was rumored, some captured German nurses from the Great Patriotic War, were harnessed and forced to run for the amusement of Kalikastani tribesmen. When the Russian gangsters took over, it was just natural to continue the tradition.

In the beginning, the sport was informal and training haphazard. Once real money started getting into it, and large sums began being wagered, naturally the sport had to become regulated. And once the sport of pony racing became institutionalized, it was just a small step to codifying the enslavement of all the other pretty Western women who had started to find themselves 'imported' into the country.

One of the principal rules that had been agreed upon early was that the women who would be purloined into the country for purposes of enslavement would come from other than the two great nations that lay to the north and east. The idea that their sisters and daughters were serving as sexual slaves right next door would be a little to much to expect the rulers of those countries to bear. So it was decided that the females of Russia and the Ukraine would be largely off limits. That left, of course, the entire rest of the globe and there were always plenty of criminal organizations willing to facilitate the deportation of their countrywomen for the right price.

So the unhappy, pretty, young women who were kneeling at Drabik's feet, wondering whether they would see the next dawn, were not destined for the slave centers of Kalikastan. There was a more than adequate market for them abroad. They would be a welcome sweetener for Drabik's ally in his bid to unseat Grobgy, Mikhail, who dealt in that sort of thing. For Drabik did need allies. It was one thing to knock off the aging, former KGB policeman, it would be another to keep his criminal empire together. Drabik needed to ensure the loyalty of Grobgy's important lieutenants in order to secure his assumption of leadership. Hence his need for money. It was ironic that Grobgy's downfall was to be funded from his own coffers. This was Drabik's third knockoff of the day, the other two having netted him over 2 million. Another 2 million here and he had all that he would need.

The fact that it had been so easy was proof that the old man was slipping. These incompetents needed to be weeded out anyway. There were smarter, harder, more efficient men just waiting for promotion whose way had been barred by Grobgy's reliance on his old cronies. A number of hardened men from Drabik's old regiment were ready, willing and able to step in. Those who would never forgive the deposing of their old boss had to go.

The partying men and women had been surprised to see Drabik standing there with his Tokarev semiautomatic pistol lowered and aimed at them. One of the men made a move for his cannon, but Drabik dropped him easily. He forced the remaining partiers to kneel on the edge of the loading platform while he asked the men, one by one, where the money and dope was. The first two, to their credit, told him to go fuck himself. But the third, seeing his associates take nose dives onto the macadam below with life ending bullets in the back of their heads, had pissed himself and told Drabik all that he wanted to know. He had the fellow tie the women's wrists and feet together and then lead him to the treasure. When he had resumed his kneeling position at the edge of the platform, crying and sobbing, begging to be allowed to change sides and join him, Drabik had finished him off too. There was no room in Drabik's organization for men who pissed their pants.

But what to do with the third woman? They were all shapely and beautiful. And none could be left behind as witnesses.

The first one, on the end closest to Drabik, was a diminutive, little girl, with wild, puffed out chestnut brown hair, brown, well tanned skin and two large, gold, hooped earrings. Although short in stature, she was well filled out but not plump. She was wearing a tight, short, black, spandex skirt and a red, strapless, stretch, halter top that outlined her rotund breasts quite pleasingly. Her pleasant brown eyes saved her from cheapness and she had full, succulent lips which she kept licking nervously.

Next to her, was a tall, lanky blond girl. Her bright yellow hair looked like it had been dyed and was close cropped and done up in tiny ringlets. She had been on the lap of one of the men when Drabik had come in and he had been fondling her firm, round, coffee cup sized breasts. Her silken, gold colored blouse was still undone and her braless breasts were invitingly displayed. The tips were conical and her long, magenta colored nipples were stiff with her fear. They were so dark in contrast to her pale skin that Drabik wondered if she had applied makeup to them in anticipation of their use today. She was wearing a brown, leather miniskirt that came up to the middle of her long, graceful thighs. The girl's lips were thin and she kept them firmly pressed together in anticipation of what looked like her probable demise while her tear filled, pretty, blue eyes looked at him forlornly.

The third girl was a dark haired beauty, with straight, short, black hair that reached just above her shoulders. She had painted her full lips a bright red to match the sparkly red and gold blouse that she wore. Her skirt was made of shiny, fire engine red vinyl and was just long enough for decency. Her skin was dark and Drabik thought that he detected some gypsy blood in her. Her black eyes stared at him fiercely, belying the trembling of her body as she awaited his pleasure. Her plump breasts jutted out from her chest, forced outwards by the binding of her wrists behind her.

All of the girls had clearly come to party and all were, in Drabik's estimation, undoubtedly professionals. Well, professionals had to accept the hazards of their profession and hanging around with gangsters had its risks. Meeting up with people like him was one of them.

Drabik wanted more time to make up his mind as to which two he would take with him and so he ordered the women to, lie down flat on the cement floor. He went down the line of them and tied off their ankles to their wrists. He went to the filing cabinets near a large, wooden desk in the corner of the large open space and found in the bottom drawer a large roll of clear, plastic packing tape. Returning to the women, he tore off a seven inch long swath for each of them and covered their mouths with it.

It only took a few minutes for Drabik to back his large, black Mercedes into the warehouse through the loading bay door. He closed it behind him and opened the trunk. After he had retrieved the large suitcase full of cash and the smaller valise containing the kilogram of heroin that the men had had stashed, he placed them in the back of the trunk, as far up against the divider that separated it from the rear seat as he could. He took a look at the space that was remaining. It would be tight for even two of them. Three was impossible.

The tall, muscular, dark browed man trudged up the dirty, cement stairs to the three bound and gagged, unhappy women. The blond girl must have sensed that the final chapter in the day's harrowing events was drawing near since she began to sob heavily. Her despair was contagious and the other two women began to cry as well.

Drabik released their hogties, freed their ankles and brought them all back to their knees. Time was growing short and he knew that the longer he stayed in the warehouse, the more likely one of the gang's other members would happen by. So he knew that he had to make his decision. He stepped to the flouncy haired, smaller girl and lifted her halter top up over her breasts. The girl looked up at him miserably and gave a little squeal. The killer passed his hands over the luscious mounds enjoyably. It would be a shame to waste these lovely orbs, Drabik thought as he appreciated the feel of the spongy, firm flesh. He wondered what her pussy looked like and he pulled her spandex skirt up around her waist.

She was wearing a black cotton thong and he pulled it down her thighs. Her brown bush was nicely trimmed and her thighs joined her belly sweetly. He could just imagine taking possession of her pretty slit and burying his cock inside it. He crouched down in front of the girl and ran his hand over her smooth, flat belly and down over the front of her pussy. She was a keeper all right. Men would pay a lot to have the pixie-like girl at their beck and call, to own her almost child sized body that was commingled with such enticing womanhood.

He moved to the blond. Of the three, she was the prettiest. Her long body was curvaceous and elegant. He lifted her skirt and took in the sight of her naked, sparsely covered sex. She had come dressed for action, a good indication of her eagerness to perform her job. Doubtless, she would make an energetic and obedient slave.

The third girl tried to pull away as Drabik started to unbutton her blouse. He grabbed her by her hair and slapped her viciously across the face. Seizing her blouse at the top by her neck, he ripped it down the front, causing the buttons to fly every which way. She was wearing a lacy, black bra that cupped her delectable breasts but left her thick, short nipples free. Her areolas were wide and dark, almost brown. She was mewing behind her gagged lips as he pulled up her skirt to see a pair of matching panties. When he pulled them down, a thick, black, wild bush of pubic hair emerged. She was a wild one all right. Someone would have a lot of fun taming her. But was she worth the trouble? When Drabik looked back into her eyes and saw the hatred and passion pouring out of them he decided she was.

Drabik stood and addressed the unhappy women. "I can't take you all and I can't leave anyone behind." He had pulled his pistol from his shoulder holster and had clicked back the hammer. The girls all jumped at the sound of his weapon being made ready. "You," he said, pointing the weapon at the gypsy girl. "Get up and get in the trunk of my car. If you don't do what I say, I'll drop you in a second. Do you understand?"

The girl nodded affirmatively although Drabik sensed that obeying his command was the last thing that she wanted to do. On the other hand, he had made it clear that disobeying him was, in fact, the last thing that she would do.

Her loose red and gold blouse flowing around her torso, her lacy black panties still around her knees, the girl walked as quickly as she could, shuffling her feet down the steps to the well of the loading area and, taking one last hate filled look at him, climbed, not without some difficulty, into the trunk. Drabik turned back to look at the other erotically displayed women. They looked back at him fearfully, hopeful that their charms had proved sufficient to make the cut.

In the end, it was the tits that did it. The brown haired girl was better stacked and that was where the money went. The blond was more to Drabik's taste. Her body would be a pleasure to ride and she would be a pleasure to look at as she stood languidly, dressed in just a pair of high heels and wearing tight fitting slave bracelets and a collar, awaiting a command from her master. But, like the merchandisers who spread their consumer wares all round for the public to buy, Drabik chose the lowest common denominator. It would take a man of refined tastes to appreciate the apparently lustful, blond girl. But the short, more voluptuous, brown haired girl would please all of the rest.

When Drabik tapped the pixie like brown haired girl on her shoulders and instructed her to join her friend, the blond girl broke out into a long, loud wail. The killer watched the tiny girl shuffle down the stairs and then scurry to the car and hop over the bumper and into the trunk. Clearly she didn't want to wait until the man, who she had seen kill four men without a single qualm, changed his mind. Both of the chosen women's pretty, unhappy, but relieved faces peered up at him as he pressed the button on the car's keychain and the trunk slowly and automatically closed over them.

Drabik turned his attention to the blond girl. Tears were flowing down her face. It was a shame to have to waste her, he thought. The thought of her pretty breasts and lightly shrouded love lips made his cock begin to rise. Maybe he could take her if he had her ride in the front seat with him. It was a big risk. He would have to be sure of her obedience. A sampling of her talents would make up his mind.

The girl was bent over, her head to the floor. Drabik tapped her on the head with the snout of his pistol. "Get up," he ordered her curtly. She looked up at him disconsolately and, seeing the steel in his eyes, obeyed. Her whole body was shuddering with the force of her sobbing.

"I'll give you one chance," the cruel man said. "I'm going to let you suck my cock. If you do a good job and make me believe that you won't give me any trouble, I'll take you with me. Otherwise, you're going to join your friends down there on the floor. Do you understand?"

The girl nodded her head fervently, eager to do anything that would prolong her life. Drabik ripped the tape off that had covered her lips. She gave a little shriek as the skin was torn around them. Not a good sign.

"Shut the fuck up, cunt!" Drabik yelled at her. "That's one mark against you already!" The girl's face cringed in unhappiness at her mistake. Her lips tightly pursed together, she nodded her understanding to him.

Drabik lowered his fly and pulled his already hardened cock from his pants. The girl looked at it anxiously and then back up at his face. Her skittishness nearly caused Drabik to forget the whole thing when she finally took the initiative and crawled closer to him. Leaning over, she opened her mouth and took his manhood within.

She was an accomplished, experienced cocksucker. The girl lavished her tongue over the head of his shaft as she sucked delicately at it, her lips nestled just below the glans.

She pressed her head forward slowly, her lips tightly encompassing his flesh as she took it deeply within her. Drabik moaned as he felt her mouth's heat transferred to him. He could hear her sniffle and moan as she serviced him, desperately giving him the benefit of all of her skills and experience. Her bound hands twisted behind her. Her leather skirt was still pulled up around her waist and her trim, pale rear mounds were presented to view. Slowly, she drew her blond head back and forth pleasuring his stiff meat. As he felt his passions rising, Drabik tilted his head back, closed his eyes to slits, placed his hands on her soft, bright yellow head and sighed.

The girl's mouth was sensitive and she slowed each time that she felt that Drabik was about to reach his climax. She prolonged his pleasurable agony as long as she could. Drabik groaned loudly when his cock began to throb and pulse in her mouth. She sucked at him fiercely, drawing out all of his spunk as she continued to stroke his pole with her tight lips. The killer gripped her head tightly as the pleasure of his pulsing meat tore through him. He thrust his hips at the girl's mouth fervently as his jism spurted into her eager mouth, each spasm of his cock delivering a wave of fierce pleasure to his body and mind.

When his cock ceased its ejaculations, the girl continued to slurp and lick at it until she was sure that every aftershock of the harsh man's climax had faded. It was as if she didn't really want it to end. As long as the man's passions were raised, as long as he derived pleasure from her lips, she could be sure of life. When he was done with her, then, and only then, she realized, she would know whether his promise to let her live was a lie.

Drabik had placed his pistol back in his shoulder holster while the girl was servicing him. He drew it again now, cocking the hammer back and placing the business end of it against her forehead. The girl's eyes looked at him agonizingly, pleadingly. Her mouth was down turned, her cum covered lips trembling. He could see that her mind was desperately trying to decide whether a plea for life would avail her.

"Okay," Drabik finally said to her harshly. "You can come with me. But there will be two absolute, ironclad rules. One is that you will remain completely silent at all times. If I hear even a squeak out of you, I'll pull over and blow your brains out right there and then. Got it?"

Tears of relief began to cascade from the girl's eyes. She nodded eagerly.

"Second," Drabik continued, "you'll do exactly as I say, to the letter. If I feel that you're even thinking about running away or giving me trouble, you'll be dead in an instant. Understand?"

The girl moaned in fear and shook her head up and down, gripping her thin lips together tightly. For a moment, Drabik reconsidered. It was stupid to take her. She was just a cunt and there were thousands of them out there. Her fear would be plain on her face everywhere they went. It was a six hour drive to Mikhail's. There would be plenty of chances for her to make trouble, even if she didn't want to. In a second, it could be over, and no one would know about the promise he had given her.

But then he thought of her long, elegant, soft body. It would be nice to have it at his disposal after he finished his long drive. And he did promise.

Drabik was unused to indecision. It was uncharacteristic of him. And to hesitate to snuff out a life when it was in his clear interests to do so was not like him. Was his infatuation with the ponygirl changing him? He needed to be sure of himself in the next few weeks. Hesitation could cost him his life. If Grobgy even suspected that he was making a move against him it would be all over. His finger twitched on the trigger of his pistol, still pointed at the middle of the girl's forehead. She must have detected his indecisiveness since her look of hope turned suddenly into a frown. But, to her credit, she said nothing. He had laid out the rules and she was obeying him. That was a good sign. Maybe there had been enough killing here today. Four of the men had been unknown to Drabik, but one of them, the leader, he had known well, had shared drinks with him, and pussy too. Enough was enough.

"Turn around," Drabik ordered the girl. Suppressing a cry, the girl turned and presented her back to him. Drabik pulled his long, broad knife from its sheath at his side and cut the bonds that had been encircling her wrists. "Go get your and your friends' purses," he ordered her. While she ran to the table, Drabik went over too and poured himself several inches of vodka in a glass. It felt good going down his throat. He realized that his flaccid cock was still sticking from his pants and he shoved it back in and zippered up. The girl had the three small, flashy pocketbooks in her hands and stood in front of him expectantly. Her blouse was still open and her skirt was still raised around her waist. She was smart. He had not ordered her to restore her clothing and she had not. Drabik admired her lovely, compact breasts and her soft sexual folds. She had given him a damned fine blowjob. He poured another glass of the clear, harsh liquid and offered it to her. "Drink it," he commanded.

The girl looked at him gratefully, picked up the glass and tossed the vodka down her throat. It had been a tough afternoon for them both.

CHAPTER TWO
GROBGY GETS SOME NEWS

Lightning strained at her tight, confining, leather harness as she took her third lap around the long, finely groomed, dirt track at top speed. Sweat was pouring down her body in rivulets and her back and thigh muscles were straining. Her long, bare, muscular legs dug her shin high, black, leather boots deeply into the turf at each agonized step. Her free and naked breasts swayed and jerked. Her useless hands bound behind her were gripped tightly into fists and her lungs ached and begged for oxygen.

Grobgy's star ponygirl, the former Maddy Burnham, had been working out all morning. Her driver, the dwarfish, cruel man in whose custody she had been over the last few weeks snapped his lash out at her and called out his insistence, "Nezoi! Nezoi!"

The tall, strong, young, American ponygirl knew about sixty or so words in Russian. This was one of them, one repeated often to her, especially on race day. "Faster! Faster!"

But today was not a racing day. It was the midseason break, halfway through. All the racing ponies were given five days off to rest aching, weary muscles, to catch up on sleep after all the long drives between meets and so that their specially designed, brightly decorated carts and carriages could be repaired and maintained. But that did not mean idleness and Jerzi was determined to build up his charge's strength and endurance.

Lightning pulled a one pony sulky. Sulkies were the Alfa Romeos of the racing circuit. Other ponies pulled six pony broughams, four pony cabs, a three pony troika. Yearlings, ponies new to their bits, pulled a two pony trap. The showcase event of ponygirl racing was the nine pony cabriolet, an endurance race of 6000 meters where only the strongest and best trained ponies competed.

Her race was the 3000 meter, two times around the track. If sulkies were the Alfa Romeo of the sport, the three thousand meter was the Grand Prix. It was the premier race, the last event on the card at every meet.

The nearly exhausted pony did not question why she was being driven an extra lap at race speed. Ponygirls had not the right to question anything, even if they had the means to do so. The harsh bit she wore in her mouth while harnessed to a cart and the stifling, thick plug of leather that she wore at all other times made the formation of any understandable oral communications impossible. But more than that, during the brief periods when her mouth was free, when she was on her knees and a master's stiff cock was presented to her for pleasuring, or when she was allowed to consume her gruelish, plain, but nutritious meals from a bowl set on the ground, to utter a word was unthinkable. Lightning had seen a ponygirl punished once for speaking. It had been an all afternoon affair and all the other ponygirls had been assembled so that they could watch. By now, seven months into Lightning's captivity, it would practically take a red hot iron to force the pony to render the simplest word from her lips.

But even though her life was harsh, Lightning had found solace and a reason for existence in ponygirl racing.

She had determined that she would be the best and had directed all of her considerable force of will to that task. She thrilled to hear the crowds chant her name in Russian, "Molnya! Molnya! Molnya!", the same word that was inscribed in three inch high, bright blue, tattooed Cyrillic letters on her chest, as she dug deeply into herself to bring her blue and gold covered head first across the finish line.

Last season, in the spring, Lightning had taken the 1500 meter sulky championship. She had come out of nowhere, having replaced the regular 1500 meter sulky pony halfway into the first part of the season. That pony, to Lightning's owner's dismay, had pulled a ligament and Lightning was put in to replace her. To everyone's surprise, after a rough beginning, Lightning had brought home the gold.

It was highly unusual for a yearling like Lightning to run the sulky. Usually at least a full year of training was considered necessary to develop the speed and fitness to run it. As usual for yearlings, she had been running the two pony trap with her partner and lover Persephone under the firm but kind supervision of her expert driver. It had been a comparative paradise for the newly minted ponygirl. To be away from the ponybarn and the abuse that she had experienced in her initial training was a relief. No one but their drivers could whip or partake of the sexual favors of a ponygirl during racing season. They had to be totally in tune with their drivers and free from other distractions.

When Lightning was reassigned, she went from heaven to hell. The four foot tall, dark haired, callous dwarf, Jerzy Gromyko, who took her over didn't believe in coddling ponygirls. She suffered a cruel regimen of whippings and beatings under his tutelage. Worst of all, she was denied the benefits of sexual release except on days in which she had won a race.

If there was anything that ameliorated the dehumanized state to which the former young women who were converted to ponygirls were reduced it was their frequent sexual use. From virtually the moment of their awakening in the ponybarn every morning, to when they were bedded down at night, their bodies were subjected to the use of the men who worked them, the trainers, the stable hands and whoever else happened to have an urge to possess them. Of course, not every act of sexual usage resulted in the delivery of a mind and body wrenching orgasm to their bodies. Some of the men could care less if the ponygirl experienced pleasure. But most of the men enjoyed witnessing the throes of a ponygirl in orgasmic delight, their squeals and moans of pleasure, the shuddering of their graceful, hard, muscular bodies. And it was a poor trainer indeed who did not ensure that his pony enjoyed several climaxes a day.

But Jerzy believed that depriving a pony of its pleasures, while at the same time driving it frequently to unsatisfied lust, made it all the more willing to give that extra ounce of strength needed to become a winner. When the only source of pleasure was taken away, its restoration would become an obsession. For when they won, he would pleasure them long and hard after they returned to the ponygirl encampment. Jerzy had driven quite a few champions in his day. His methods, although cruel, produced results. Who could argue with success?

Lightning continued her sprint around the track even though she was nearing the depletion of her resources. It was said that, unless ordered to halt, a ponygirl would run itself into the ground before stopping. Lightning was no different, but that did not prevent her from praying that the order to halt would come soon. She dreaded the awful torment that she would suffer if she were to disappoint her driver. And in front of all the watching people too!

The hood that Lightning wore was divided into hemispheres of blue and gold, the dividing line passing down the middle of where her face would have been. It covered her whole face and neck. It was made of a specially fabricated Neoprene and it stretched tightly over her head and face to remove all traces of humanity. There were little, dime sized holes for her eyes, allowing her to see just enough of what she needed to see to obey her masters' commands. It had an opening for her nostrils and a wide opening for her mouth so that a gag, a leather covered steel bit or a cock could be inserted. Under the hood, her head was completely shaved but for a skein of hair allowed to dangle out the back in a long, well groomed ponytail. She wore a wide, stiff leather covered plastic collar that held her chin upwards. When she tilted forwards to run, her head would be poised at just the right angle so that she could see down the track ahead of her.

Dangling down the back of the collar was a long, wide leather strap. For seven months, Lightning's hands had been almost continuously affixed to this strap, one above the other, just above the waistline. Since she slept on her back, chained to the floor of the ponybarn, having the arms one above the other rather than crisscrossed eased her posture. And having the hands hang loosely behind her eased the strain on her shoulders and made her less conscious of her bound arms. Lightning now barely thought of them as part of her.

The straining pony came around the near turn and could see the finish line ahead. She desperately hoped that her sprint would end there. Her heart was pounding and her legs were beginning to feel like they were made of lead. The lack of sufficient oxygen to fuel her blood was making her dizzy. She barely took notice of the nattily dressed men and women strewn along the outside rail of the track. Her driver had drawn the attention of the visitors to the track today when he started her on her sprint. Although it was not a race day, it was customary to allow members of the public to attend the third day of the rest period to gawk and stare at the ponies as they were put through their paces. More than a few of the attendees were touts, come to see what condition Grobgy's teams were in. Grobgy had won the overall estate championship in the spring and he was favored to win it again. He was already ahead of his nearest rival by fourteen points.

The wide, well groomed track lay before an elegant grandstand. On race day it would be filled with patrons eager to take in the thrill of watching naked, well trained and physically pleasing, former women lead their carriages and carts along the track. Betting was di riguer, for it was, after all, a sporting event. Having a few kronskis on the outcome made it all the more exciting. There were heavy betters too and more than one family's nest egg had been torn up and thrown on the ground when the favored pony lost.

The nearly spent pony felt like she was about to collapse when she finally gained the finish line. She waited, hopefully for the special signal communicated through the reins affixed to her bit that would allow her to slow down. In the hands of an expert driver, which Jerzy was, all kinds of things could be conveyed to a pony through the long, thick, leather straps. Stop, slow down, speed up, speed up faster, right, left, canter, prance, back up, these were all commands that a well trained pony could divine from the expert handling of its reins, especially from a driver with whom it was well acquainted. By now, there was no driver with whom Lightning was more well acquainted than the devilish Jerzy.

Jerzy, sitting crouched and intent in his spring supported seat, was resplendent in his racing day uniform. On practice days, he usually wore a simple peasant style shirt and jeans together with a well worn pair of dark brown work boots. Today, although not a race day, was a show day and all the drivers had donned their racing duds for the benefit of the onlookers. His shirt and pants were made from shiny blue and gold silk to match the racing hood worn by his pony. He wore a jockey's cap of similar make and color and tall, almost luminous, black boots.

The sulky cart was polished and primped for the visual pleasure of the audience as well. The two, large wheels were made of fine polished oak and steel with blue and gold ribbons intertwined in the spokes. A blue and gold pennant emblazoned with the heraldic symbol of the Grobgy estate fluttered from its back. All of the estates adopted symbols reminiscent of chivalric escutcheons and the middle ages as their totems. Grobgy's was a fierce, yellow, rampant, snarling wolf, and it appeared on the flags and pennants that surrounded the racing track and was mounted atop the grand stand just below the Kalikastani national flag, which had three wide stripes on it, red, blue and gold, with a large, black, mailed fist in the center. On racing day, the flag of the visiting estate would be flown as well.

Lightning also bore the dreaded symbol of the ruthless gangster. It was customary to tattoo on the flat, trim bellies of the new ponies the emblem of their training estate. Just above her naked and exposed, hairless nether lips, Lightning bore a large yellow, tattooed rendition of the angry wolf. Some estates, like Grobgy's, trained ponies for the open market, and it was not unusual for a pony with Grobgy's mark on its belly to be running for another estate. The true indicia of ownership of a ponygirl was carried on its loins in the form of two golden disks that were attached to its lower nether lips. The symbol of its owner and the pony's name were etched on them.

The ponygirl driver knew that Lightning was at the end of her rope. He knew the pony well. But he was determined not to let her decide when she should stop. They passed the finish line at near top speed, the best that could be expected after three, long laps, and he let her continue down the track for another thirty meters before giving the reins a little flick that denoted that she could ease up.

A light round of applause came from the other side of the four foot high, white, railed fence that separated the onlookers from the track. Jerzy acknowledged the appreciation of the small crowd with a tip of his cap as he encouraged his pony into her cool down lap. Her back and rear haunches were shiny with sweat and he could tell from her slight weaving that she had almost reached her breaking point. "Good," he thought. It was good to make the pony exceed her limits. There was almost always something else to give and his charge had just discovered a whole new well of reserve to draw upon.

Jerzy had another reason to put on the display of what might be called 'horsemanship'. He knew that the gambling professionals and scouts for the other estates were watching. Seeing Lightning run full throttle an extra 1500 meters would befuddle their racing strategies against her. Should they have their ponies start strong and try and run the blue and gold hooded pony down? Not a likely strategy if she could keep up the pace that she had just shown for 4500 meters. Well, how about laying back and overtaking her with a burst of speed at the end? Lightning had just shown them how deep her reserve of strength was. No, the only way to beat Lightning, at least while he was driving her, was to have a stronger, faster, more determined pony. Jerzy doubted that such a pony existed.

Lightning was blubbering as she strained her chest to pull in enough oxygen to overcome her anaerobic deficit. Since her mouth was largely blocked by the cruel bit that she wore, she had to take in most of her air through her nose. It was a trick that new ponies took a while to learn. Her mind was reeling with the fever of her recent effort. The only thought that she could manage was whether or not she had pleased her cruel caretaker and driver. If not, she could expect a good half hour with the whip when she got back to camp. Maybe, if she had done really well, he would let her suck him off. She missed the thrill of a hot, throbbing cock in her mouth. It made her wet just to think about it.

Sucking a cock was about the only chance that a ponygirl had to take an active role in her use. Once in a while, one of the masters let a pony get on top and stroke his cock with her well trained, eager sleeve. But usually they took their fucking from behind while posed against a rail or maybe sprawled in the dirt with their strong, long legs pushed up to their shoulders. Lightning liked it when they made her kneel, her breasts crushed against her thighs and mounted her from behind. But the ability to control the masters' sexual pleasure, to prolong their ecstasy until, overcome with their urgency, they grabbed her long, silken ponytail and pressed her face to their loins, gave her a feeling of power, something wholly lacking in any other phase of her life as a virtual beast.

It took a good five minutes for the ponygirl to trot around the track and back to the starting line. The crowd had thinned, but there were still a number of admirers waiting. Lightning heard the heavy rumbling of the nine pony team passing her on the left. Most of the teams were out today and they shared the track, taking turns performing their heats. Her legs and shoulder muscles were starting to recover from her ordeal and they felt loose and weary, a good kind of weary, the kind that let you know that you could do it again tomorrow if you had to. She didn't mind the hard training. In fact, she reveled in it. It was the only way that she could maintain her edge. She wanted another gold medal to wear on her collar, a sign of her superiority over the other ponygirls. If she had to be a ponygirl, and there didn't seem to be any real likelihood that she would ever be anything else, she wanted to be outstanding, not an anonymous, hooded animal.

Jerzy stopped the cart just past the finish line to let the gawkers get a good look at the ponygirl champion. No pictures were allowed. No one wanted a photograph of a ponygirl on the front page of the New York Times. Ponygirl racing was a good thing that would be spoiled if too much publicity about it got out. Oh, the Western security agencies knew all about it. You really couldn't keep a thing like this secret, but the trade offs of having a 'free fire zone' like Kalikastan more than offset their qualms about how a small number of their former citizens were treated, a miniscule number when compared to the millions left untouched. The country was crawling with agents and their minions, all looking to trade or buy information, transfer secret funds, smuggle weapons and technology.

And while you were there, you could partake of the many benefits of female sexual slavery. Kalikastan was a favored vacation spot for the world's underworld. As long as you kept your activities within the bounds of propriety, shoot outs and assassinations while 'in country' were frowned upon by the criminal National Commission that ran the place, you could enjoy yourself, take in a race or two, and torment a pretty, subservient slave girl to your heart's content.

The only time that Lightning became self conscious of her continuous nudity was when she was displayed, as she was now, to the eyes of 'outsiders', as she thought of them. Dressed in their finery, even the young girls would ogle and joke about the naked and hairless former women. Lightning's chest was still heaving slightly and she could feel her ample breasts sway and jiggle with the effort. She had yearned and pined desperately for freedom in the first weeks after her conversion. Alone at night in the ponybarn, after a day of cruel, harsh training and an evening of sexual abuse, she would cry and wail until the night watchman would come by and give her a stroke of his whip to silence her. She had come to terms since then with her fate. But standing still as an object of curiosity, her nakedness and tattooed marks of enslavement brazenly displayed to what were ordinary, regular, everyday people made her cringe with shame.

The dwarf was well aware of how ponygirls reacted to being put on display. In his estimation, it was good for them. It brought home in a direct way their separation from the world of human beings. And it emphasized the hopelessness of their fate. No one was going to help them. No one cared that they had once been independent, self determined women. Not a thought was given to the injustice of depriving them of all attributes of personhood. They were ponies now and that was that.

The four foot high man hopped off of his seat and down to the track. He carried with him a plastic bottle of fortified water. It had a long straw attached so that it could be poked over the top of the pony's bit and allow it to drink. Lightning was more than a foot and a half taller than him and so he gave his fingers a snap and the pony compliantly sank to her knees in her traces. He pushed the straw into her mouth, squeezed the bottle and gave her a long, refreshing drink.

It was difficult for Lightning to absorb all of the revitalizing flow at once and remnants dribbled down over her lips and chin and spilled over her chest and breasts. The liquid gave her pretty, plump mounds an attractive sheen and Jerzy could not resist giving them a caress with his small but steel strong hands. Lightning knelt obediently in the dust as he massaged her orbs to the delight of the small crowd. She felt him tickling her nipples, raising them to stiffness and heard the amused sounding comments in Russian from the people across the rail from her. She could not turn her head to see them; the reins that led out from the sides of her bit had been tied off tightly by her driver before he dismounted the cart and she was unable to move her head more than a few inches in either direction. Jerzy snapped his fingers again and the pony dutifully rose to her feet. The small man ran his hands over her belly and hips and then delved his hand between her thighs and began to stroke her smooth, hairless nether lips.

The feel of the man's hand on her sex sent an involuntary shudder through the distraught ponygirl. She knew that the man could drive her to intense arousal at will and she was shamed to be so handled in front of the fascinated people. But the pony had little control over her reactions and to resist his manhandling of her needy loins was unthinkable. As his fingers worked the slit between her engorging labia, Lightning gave a little sigh of distress and spread her thighs obediently to give the hand more room. Shame ran through her as she had a mental picture of herself standing there, her body harnessed firmly to the cart, naked and hooded, her hands bound behind her.

Her fleshy purse had lubricated and Lightning could feel the tiny fingers of the man gain admission to the soft, moist interior while his thumb worried the hardened nub at its top. Her blood was beginning to get hot and she could sense her arousal growing higher and higher. Her body wanted completion, wanted the thrilling, hard contractions of her pussy to send it wave after wave of pleasure. But her mind did not. She didn't want to come in front of the merry, strange people laughing and joking insensitively at her plight.

Her driver had resumed the manipulation of her blood filled breasts with his free hand, accelerating the pony's excitement. The former American college student gave out a moan as her crisis approached. Her mind had overridden her objections to being so callously handled and she began to fervently hope that the man would bring her to delight, crowd or no crowd. What did it matter really, she thought.

Who was she to have pride or sensibilities? This was what she was now, an object of amusement and sport, her whole body, with its garish tattoos, her bindings, her nakedness, advertised it. The most expressive part of her face, her eyes, was effectively hidden behind the tiny dots that served as her portal to the world. To the onlookers, she was sure she looked like she was enjoying herself, another happy ponygirl demonstrating her lascivious nature.

Jerzy pondered whether to allow the pony an orgasm. It would be amusing for the crowd, something they could tell their friends. He knew that she was nearing her crisis, her chest had broken out in a bright pink, her breasts were hard and she had begun to pant. Her pussy was loose and wet and he could feel her pushing it back at his hand. Why not, he thought. Today was all about public relations and giving the people a show was good for the sport. And it was good for the pony too to demonstrate to her once more her lack of control of her own sexuality. He determined where and when she could come.

Lightning moaned as her orgasm struck her. Her knees buckled and her body swayed as her pussy sent wave after wave of pleasure through her. She pressed her hips forward seeking to encourage the hand that was tormenting her. Her mind was overwhelmed with the electrified sensations her cunt was sending it even as it flooded with shame at the sound of the crowd laughing and shouting with delighted approval at her display.

The dwarf enjoyed the feel of the luxuriantly flush sexual canal of the ponygirl. Her moans of pleasure and the shuddering of her enticing, sweat covered body as a result of her forced orgasm were amusing. But Jerzy didn't want to linger long. The pony needed a rub down and, perhaps, the whip. He hadn't decided yet whether to reward her with his cock for her near Herculean effort or to beat her for not doing better. He would decide when they got back to the camp. Satisfied that he had obtained the last gasp of pleasure from the former woman, he eased his musk covered fingers from her sopping pussy and, after giving her breasts a final squeeze, hopped back onto the cart. He gave a slight snap on her reins and she instantly responded by going into motion. He could sense that she was still dazed from her lustful experience, but he knew that she would recover quickly.

Jerzy had her make a wide turn and, after trotting about thirty meters down the track in the opposite direction from which she had been running, he brought her full circle so that she could pass before the full line of onlookers. He signaled the pony to shift into her high kicking prance, her knees lifted high, each step deliberate and stylish, her beauteous breasts bouncing merrily. Her long, fine, chestnut colored ponytail jerked and swayed behind her. As the pony obediently danced before the small crowd, he lifted his cap again and waived it to another round of applause. When the pony reached the end of the grandstand, he snapped the reins and Lightning, happy that the show was over, her body still tingling from her sexual release, obediently resumed her trot. Today's work was done.

* * * * * * * * * * * * * *

Up in the grandstand, in the owner's box, Axmail Grobgy was having quite a laugh. He had seen the erotic display put on by Jerzy with his favorite ponygirl and it amused him. On his left sat his beautiful and corrupt young daughter Anya. She was laughing too. But Lightning was far from her favorite ponygirl. In fact, Anya had every reason to despise the statuesque, voluptuous pony.

Anya and Drabik had been lovers for quite a long time. It was not something that was well advertised. Her father kept a close watch on his only child, not a child really, but a sexually hyperactive 22 year old vixen. She was allowed free reign with the ponygirls and ubiquitous slave girls. Grobgy didn't mind that. After all, everyone needed a sexual outlet or two. But he drew the line at male lovers. Several of those who had assumed the role as Anya's beau were fertilizing the steppes now. He would pick her suitor. Whoever became her mate would be the presumptive heir of his criminal empire and he wanted to make sure that it was someone who could survive the inevitable power struggle. And there was the fact that whoever fucked his daughter would feel like he had one over on the unscrupulous criminal boss. No one had that right.

So Anya and Drabik met secretly in a small inn some thirty kilometers away from the estate in an upstairs room whenever they could get away, which wasn't often enough for the tall, lithe, black haired beauty. And then Lightning had come along.

Anya knew of the killer's obsession with the ponygirl. It wasn't natural and she was at a loss at how to fight it. She had tried. She had shamed Drabik into administering a ferocious beating to the defenseless former woman. She had taunted and beat her herself. She even played the ponygirl now for Drabik, letting him adorn her in the accouterments of a pony, a hood, the boots, the gag, and let him bind her wrists behind her and fuck her mouth as he would a cunt. She had been surprised at how deliriously exciting the experience was. The first time that he had used her ass, she had exploded into orgasm.

But nothing she did served to dilute his passion for the ponygirl champion. She had seen him sneaking down to the pony barn to fuck her before the fall racing season started and she became off limits. At least then they had been able to return to their routine. She couldn't shake the feeling, however, that he was using her body as a substitute for the other, that when he looked at her hooded head and pressed his thick cock past her welcoming lips, he wasn't thinking of her.

So it was exquisite for Anya to watch the ponygirl be humiliated before the crowd. If only she could get rid of her. Her father wouldn't sell her in a million years. If she did anything to permanently harm the creature, she might find herself shipped off to some whorehouse in Asia Minor or worse. She wouldn't put it past the old bastard. There were rumors about her mother's 'accident' many years ago. Not anything that would dare be suggested directly to her face, but things had been said and looks had been exchanged on the rare occasions that her name came up.

There was one chance. She had heard about the claiming race that the American billionaire was supposedly trying to get her father to agree to. If Lightning lost the race, her worries would be over. Drabik would be unhappy for a while, but she knew that she could make him forget her.

Grobgy looked over at his pretty, sensuous daughter. He knew about her hatred for the pony, Lightning. He knew a lot more than she knew he knew. For example, he knew all about her and Drabik. He had stopped short of having their bedroom bugged. He didn't want to know the intimate details of his daughter's sex life. He had some standards, after all. But he knew that she was fucking his right hand man.

At first, he was going to have the fearsome killer dumped into a hole. Then he thought about it. He was getting on, a little over sixty now, and Drabik was young and strong. He was ruthless and smart enough to be a powerful successor. If he was, in fact, in love with his daughter, he would protect her after he was gone. For if any one else came to power, someone who had no affinity for her, she would, if she were lucky, lie in his gave with him, a bullet in her head. If she were not lucky, well, he didn't want to think about it.

So he let them go on, for the while at least. Once the season was over, he had decided, he would make up his mind: kill the killer or make him marry his daughter.

Kneeling next to the heavyset, unscrupulous gang leader was a lithesome, brown haired slave girl. A leash led from a hook on the arm of Grobgy's chair to a ring in the middle of the shield gag that she wore over her mouth. The leather pad covered her lower face from her upper lip to her chin and had attached to it a long, thick leather plug that sat in her mouth. She was naked, as befitted a slave girl, and held her pose dutifully, her back erect, her thighs spread. Her hands were bound behind her by the leather bracelets that all of the slave girls wore and there was a leather collar around her beautiful, long neck. Her pretty, brown, limpid eyes were focused on the fearsome face of her master and new owner.

Chrissie Whitmore was fairly new to her bonds. She still rued displaying her naked, plump, round breasts to one and all and the proffering of the hairless slit between her thighs. Whenever one of the men who were sharing the luxurious, open air box overlooking the race track below looked at her, measuring her worth as an object of their lusts, she was conscious of the two inch high Cyrillic, bright, blue lettering tattooed on her chest denoting her new name, Yulia, set forth as "*Юлия*", and the snarling head of a ferocious black bear with blood red fangs and evil, red eyes etched into her belly, the emblem of her slave training house.

Yulia had been delivered to the Grobgy estate two days ago. She had undergone an intense, unforgiving course of sexual abuse and whippings for the last several weeks until she had been deemed compliant and obediently sensuous enough to put her on the open market. Grobgy's agent in Dlitski, the nation's capital, had picked her out for his boss from a line of six other compliant and naked graduating trainees. She had been trundled into a steel cage that afternoon and placed on the back of a pickup truck. She didn't know how long she had been driven or to where, since the cage had been covered with a tarp. When she arrived here, way out in the middle of nowhere as far as she was concerned, she had been taken to an office in the large, foreboding mansion and presented to the dark, black haired, bearded man at whose feet she now knelt. He had beaten her with a riding crop and then fucked her. He had apparently approved of her training and subservience since he had had her, to her dismay, at his side continuously since she had arrived.

Yulia, all of 21 years old, had followed a not too uncommon path to her slavery. She had just broken up with her boyfriend, Tom, a bright, promising engineering student. They had lived together for two years while they both attended Berkeley University. It had been great at first. Tom was a considerate, loving, boyfriend. But there was just something about him that had started to grate on her. He was very possessive and often quizzed her intently on nights when she went out with girl friends or stayed late at the library. He always seemed to be hovering over her and recently had gotten into a fight with a guy at a bar when he thought that he was trying to pick her up. The boy was in one of her classes and she was discussing that day's lecture with him. He was smaller than Tom, but handled himself pretty well and Tom had gotten the worst of it. Things just weren't the same after that.

She had told Tom that she was breaking up with him. She had packed all of her stuff and had moved it over to her girlfriend's apartment. He had been waiting for her when she got out of class late the next afternoon and had begged her to go to dinner with him so they could talk it over. Well, she felt like she owed him that at least. Over the meal at an out of the way restaurant down Highway 1, near the coast, she had stood her ground, trying to be as kind as she could. It wasn't that she hated him, it was just, well, she was only 21 after all and there were a lot of other guys out there, guys who wouldn't make her feel as if they owned her.

After the meal, Tom had told her he needed to make a stop in Oakland to pick up something from a friend. She suspected it had something to do with drugs. That was another thing that had started to bother her about Tom. A little partying was one thing, but his use of coke had gotten out of hand.

When they pulled up to the tenement building, she at first had wanted to wait in the car. But the neighborhood was so skeevey that she gave in when Tom insisted she come in. She didn't like the look the tall, heavyset black man had given her when he answered the door. She was dressed neatly in a not too tight pair of designer blue jeans, a loose, plain, white cotton blouse and a pair of comfortable, low heeled shoes. The way the man looked at her, she felt like she was wearing nothing at all. She started to get nervous when, at his lugubrious invitation, they went downstairs to the basement.

It was when they entered a large room with a cement floor covered with a thin, worn, commercial quality rug, boarded over windows and an old, battered mattress in the corner that she began to believe that something was wrong. There were three other young, rough looking, black men sitting around in ratty old chairs that looked like they had been retrieved from the curb on trash day. The room was lit by a single, dim light bulb. She could smell the odor of marijuana in the musty air and there was a little table set up with bottles of booze and glasses on it.

Chrissie had just turned to tell Tom that she would wait upstairs when her former lover delivered a resounding slap across her face. It was so unexpected she lost her balance and fell to the floor. Before she had a chance to scream, she felt his hand in her long, light brown hair and he yanked her back to her feet.

"Ow! Tom! Tom! What are you doing?" she yelled as the pain of the blow to her face and the strain on the roots of her hair coursed through her.

Tom responded with another rough slap across her face. "Shut the fuck up, you cunt!" he yelled.

"Ohhhhh!" she cried out. This time, held up by Tom's vice like grip in her locks, she kept her feet even though the blow rocked her teeth.

The young black men in the room were laughing at Tom's display.

"Hey, white boy," one of them called out, "don't damage the merchandise, okay?" The room erupted in laughter.

Tom looked at the other men with fire in his eyes and than back to Chrissie. "Say hello to your new friends, Chrissie," he told her, contempt dripping from his voice.

"What?" Chrissie answered, dumfounded. "What do you mean? What are you doing, Tom? Please...."

Tired of his former girlfriend's questions, he gave her a rude shove and she fell to the floor at the feet of the three black men who formed a semi-circle around her.

"You wanted to fuck around, Chrissie, well now you'll get your chance."

Terrified and confused, Chrissie looked up at the grinning, leering men. New friends? Did that mean what she thought it meant? The three black men were looking down at her with undisguised lust and power. This can't be happening, she thought desperately. She turned to look back at her former boyfriend. "Please don't do this Tom," she entreated pitiably. "I thought that you loved me?'

Tom's face was red with rage. "Love you? I used to love you. That was before you dumped me, Chrissie! Now you can suffer too! Have fun fucking these home boys. Maybe you'll like black cock." There was more laughter from the men.

The seeming leader of the group, a tall, thin, coffee colored man with sharp features and cruel eyes interjected jocularly in a taunting, wise-ass voice, "Yeah, Chrissie. Once you've had black, you'll never go back," he said gripping his loins with a long, caramel colored hand. The other two men, heavier and even meaner looking, were black as night. They were dressed in tattered t-shirts that went down only to the edge of their waist, leaving a three inch gap above their pants. Their pants were long and baggy and the tops of their boxer shorts peeked up above them. They all wore fancy, $350.00 sneakers.

"Goodbye, Chrissie," Tom said. "Have fun being a whore. And whenever a strange man is sticking his cock down your throat, think of me. Okay?"

Tom whirled and went out the door. It closed with a loud 'clang'.

The men kept Chrissie down in the basement room for three days. Not that Chrissie knew how long it was. The light was always on and the windows let in no light. The men came and went. She lost count of how many had used her and how many times they had forced their thick, black cocks down her throat, or pierced her now sore and cum coated nether lips. They had stripped her of her blouse and jeans and underwear and kept her wrists tied off to a steel bolt at the head of the mattress. She had fought and screamed in the beginning, but then one of them gave her a shot of something that made her woozy and relatively cooperative.

On the third day, she found herself kneeling in the middle of the room with her hands bound behind her and a hood over her head. She was weak and tired and dirty. The only time that she had left the room was when she was taken out to a bathroom down the hall. They had kept her hooded and bound then too.

Chrissie believed that the men would eventually kill her. What else could they do? She had seen all of their faces. But it did not turn out like she thought. She heard the door open and the voice of what sounded like a white man. He didn't have the cadence and rhythm of the black men's patois. She felt herself pulled to her feet and the man started feeling her body, her breasts and her belly.

"She's a fucking mess," the man said, disgusted.

"She'll clean up good," the man who Chrissie believed was the leader returned. "She fucks real good too."

"I'll bet," the white man answered. "Turn her around."

Chrisie felt her body turned so that her back was to the new voice. His hands roamed over her rear cheeks and snuck between her legs. She was too tired and depressed to complain. They could do what they wanted with her.

Then the man spoke again. "I'll give you a thousand bucks for her."

"Oh, fuck you!" the leader said, his voice rising. "This is prime beef on the hoof, my man. She's worth a lot more than that."

"Not to me she isn't," the man returned.

Chrissie's head spun. Was she being sold? For $1,000? Was that all she was worth?

"Well you can go suck on your grand, man," the black man said. "You ain't even seen her face yet."

"I don't need to see her face. She could be Princess Grace for all I care," the white man replied. "Listen," he said, "what are you going to do with her? You could put her on the street to earn, but sooner or later she'd get away and all you guys would end up doing long stretches at Folsom. Or you could cut her up and dump her somewhere. But that's a guaranteed life stretch if someone dimes you out. And sooner or later, one of your asshole buddies will get jammed up and deal you. So what are you going to do? I'm doing you a favor by taking her off of your hands."

"Shiiiit!" the black man said. He paused, obviously thinking over the other man's logic. Chrissie's stomach was roiling with fear, being between Scylla and Charybdis. Was it better to remain as the sexual plaything of these cruel, black men, who at least seemed to want to keep her alive, or go to the unknown fate represented by the mean sounding white man who had just assessed her physical attributes like he was buying some kind of domesticated animal? She just wanted to be free. She had cried many times over the last few days, begged and pleaded to be released, promising that she wouldn't tell, until the men had slapped her so hard she had stopped. But now she wanted to beg and plead again.

"Please, let me go," she whimpered under her hood. "I won't say anything, I promise. Please!"

The black man gave her a vicious slap across her breasts. "Shut the fuck up, bitch!" he yelled at her. Chrissie groaned with pain and unhappiness. She bent over to prevent another blow and fell back to her knees. She started sobbing heavily.

"Okay, okay!" the black man said. "But make it $2500. That's fair."

"I said a grand and it's a grand," the white man returned. "Otherwise I'll take my cash for the delivery and get going."

"Man, you is one cheap motherfucker!" the black man said.

"This is getting old, fella," the white man responded, unperturbed by the castigation. "Yes or no?"

"Okay, okay," the black man said. "But next time, we'll call somebody else."

"Suit yourself," the white man replied.

There was a few moments while accounts were squared during which Chrissie lamented her fate. She cursed Tom and the men who had held her prisoner, all men, everybody in the world. She couldn't imagine what the white man had in mind for her, but she was sure that she wouldn't like it.

Hands pulled Chrissie to her feet and she stood there limply while her hood was pulled off. A piece of tape was placed over her lips and the hood replaced. A strong hand grabbed her arm and she was led outside the room, up the stairs and out the back door of the house. She didn't know what time it was, but being outside was a blessing after her ordeal in the basement. She didn't even care that she was stark naked. She heard the sound of a car trunk opening and she was pushed inside. Hands bound her ankles and connected them to her already bound wrists.

The frightened young girl did not know how far she was driven, but it was a long time before she was let out. She was brought into another building and held there for several days. She never did see the face of the man who had liberated her from the drug dealers' basement. He kept her hooded and let her eat only after he had blindfolded her. She was happy though that he kept her clean and did not use her that much.

Someone else came and took her away from there and then it all just got jumbled up in her memory. She couldn't remember if she was transferred three or four more times. After her last confinement, she was placed in a long, silver tube and drugged. When she awoke, she was in Kalikastan.

It was culture shock, to say the least for a young American woman to be faced with the reality of sexual slavery. Chrissie had read about things like that in the paper, but they seemed to be happening to East European women tempted out from behind the former Iron Curtain to supposedly lucrative jobs in the West. She was dreadfully surprised at how the men all accepted it as commonplace and that they were so open about it. When she was taken to her training facility, she cried miserably after she had been tattooed, but soon realized that if she did not accept her new life, at least for the time being, she would be destroyed. She started to open herself readily, suck the cocks with abandon. She learned to excite herself when a man came to use her and to obey every command with alacrity, no matter how unhappy she was to receive it.

She had thought that she had reached the lowest level of her degradation until she had met her current owner. He was rough and callous and whipped and fucked her. That was not what had caused her new low of fear and unhappiness. Before, she had thought of herself as a captive, a prisoner. She was still herself and had will and retained a piece of her freedom in her mind. The free, callous use that the heavy set, dark man made of her was somehow different from what she had experienced before. Up till the moment she had been unhooded in his presence, she had been a creature in transition, from her old life, which now seemed centuries ago, to a new one. And here it was. Her process of transformation to a slave was complete. She was owned, less than a human being, a chattel.

Today was the first day that she had been out of the mansion. She had seen the other, pretty, naked slave girls come and go while she knelt at her master's feet in his office, while he ate in the dining room, even in his huge, luxurious bedroom. She had even watched while he had fucked some of them. But she had not been prepared for what she saw when they went down the front steps of the sprawling estate house. There, at the bottom of the steps, waiting patiently, were two hooded women, naked and in harness. They were tall and strong and had long, reddish ponytails dangling from the back of their heads. Behind them was a cart with reins attached to some kind of devices in their mouths.

Yulia, as she was now called, didn't have much time to take in the strange, disconcerting sight since her master, she didn't even know his name yet, tied off the leash that was connected to her gag to the back of the cart. She watched dolefully as he mounted it, gripped the reins and set the weirdly accoutered women into motion.

The tug of her leash told Yulia that she was to follow the cart. Her feet were bare and it hurt to run behind it to god knew where. Her hands were bound behind her and it was difficult to keep up the pace. She knew that if she fell, she would be dragged painfully along behind it and probably suffer another bout with the cruel man's whip. By the time they got to the racing track, her chest was heaving painfully and she was covered with sweat.

She followed her master dutifully, her body shining with perspiration as he led her by her leash into the large grand stand. She was amazed at the nonchalance of the well dressed, happy people as she went past them, stopping only as her master halted in response to a greeting. Other, naked slave girls were in attendance, darting to and fro carrying trays of refreshments or submissively following other masters at the end of a leash. When they arrived at the box where she now knelt, she saw for the first time the object of the attention of the people who she had seen staring out at the track. There were dozens of them, these harnessed women, and they were energetically pulling all sorts of carriages and carts along the wide dirt racing track.

"What kind of world is this?" she thought to herself. "Where am I?" She felt as if she had entered some kind of alternative universe like some of the science fiction books that she had liked to read as a teenager. Could a world like this really exist? All the people seemed so happy and merry. Didn't anyone have an ounce of pity for the poor women forced to act as some kind of ponies? If they had no scruples about what they had done to those poor women, what hope did she have? The thought occurred to her, what if they wanted to make her a ponygirl? What would she do then? It was as if a knife had pierced her heart. "Oh, Tom, Tom," she thought miserably, "how could you do this to me?"

Grobgy looked down at his new slave girl. He could see the discomfiture in her pretty eyes. He liked to break in the new girls. There was something about their terror and bewilderment at their predicament that was particularly enjoyable. This one was pretty and had screamed and cried most satisfyingly when he whipped her. He would send her down to the bunk house in a day or so so that the boys could have their fun with her, but he hadn't tired of her yet.

The crime lord leaned over and took one of the girl's plump breasts in his hand and gave it a strong squeeze. The girl's eyes winced in pain.

Just then the gangster's reverie was interrupted. One of his henchmen came up to him and whispered in his ear.

"What!" he cried out. "What!"

The unhappy messenger leaned over and repeated his message of disaster in the heavyset, cruel man's ear.

Grobgy leaped to his feet. Three of his operations back in Russia had been knocked over! How could that happen! He needed to get back to the mansion and get on the phone right away! There were no cell phones in Kalikastan. Too much of went on there was secret. And there were no phones at the grandstand, only the phone in the officials' booth so that results could be sent to the government approved bookmakers around the country. And so Grobgy had to go all the way back to the estate house to make his calls.

Yulia, who had seen plenty of her callous new owner over the last couple of days had never seen him like this. His face was a mask of rage and was turning bright red. He gave her a look of pure evil and yanked her to her feet by her leash. She stumbled helplessly after him as he dashed out of the owner's box.

Anya, too, was startled by her father's behavior. Only something of huge magnitude could pull him away from his favorite hobby. She had seen him like this before and somebody, somewhere was going to get it in the neck! She knew better than to ask or to follow him. She decided that she would make herself scarce.

Grobgy tied his slave girl's leash to the back of the ponycart. The tall, sturdy, naked ponygirls had been standing idly in their harness, dutifully awaiting whatever task was appointed to them next and were startled as he hopped onto it and gave a fierce yank of their reins. They were big boned, Irish ponies with bright orange, flowing ponytails and pale, white skin. Former racers, Grobgy used them mostly for sport although they were used from time to time to haul small loads around the estate. They jumped immediately into action

Grobgy snapped the long pony whip on their haunches as he demanded more speed from them. It was a little over a kilometer to the mansion over a winding, hilly pathway. It was no problem for the fit, experienced ponies to do it at top speed. But poor Yulia at the back was brought to the extremes of her endurance. She didn't know what news her new owner had received, but she could tell that it was bad and that his rage bode ill for her. She was frightened and exhausted when they reached the mansion and, when the cart finally halted, she doubled over to try and catch her breath. Grobgy had no inclination to allow her to recover her equilibrium and pulled her behind him rudely, practically dragging her, as he entered the house and mounted the long, broad, curved stairs that led to his private office. When he got there, he pulled the large oaken door open and, after yanking his slave girl inside, slammed it shut. He left her keeling on the floor, crying and heaving for breath as he went to the desk.

An ocean of rage was storming inside him. Four million, all gone in one day! Ten men dead! Who could have done it? Someone was making a move on him, that was clear, but who? The Bronski brothers had a running feud with him, but they were essentially just small time. Kerensky was capable of it, and so were Dublitski and Tamarov. If only Drabik was here! But he was on a mission and unreachable.

Grobgy took his arm and swept all of the things off of his desk. His lamp and the telephone went crashing to the floor together with all of his papers. He went behind his desk and picked up the chair and threw it across the room, smashing it into the wall. He needed a way to get his anger out so that he could think. Then he remembered the pretty slave girl that was kneeling at his feet.

Yulia was trembling with fear. She had never seen a man so enraged before. When the man turned to her, she knew that she was going to bear the brunt of his anger. "Mmmmmmmmmmm!" she moaned piteously. "Please, god, no," she begged in her mind.

"Get up!" Grobgy ordered her. When the girl hesitated, he stepped to her and grabbed her by the hair and lifted her to her feet. He pulled her over to a chain that hung from the ceiling in the corner of the room. He freed her hands from behind her and fastened her bracelets to the chain. She was whining and crying and she struggled as he locked one wrist and then the other above her head. "Good!" Grobgy thought. "Struggle, fight back. It'll make this all the better."

The girl pulled frantically on her fastened arms as Grobgy retreated across the room to get his whip. There were several mounted on the wall behind his desk. He pulled down a four foot long, thin, steel wand covered with leather. It would mark the girl up beautifully.

When Grobgy returned, Yulia was sobbing uncontrollably. She tried to imagine whatever in her life she could have done to deserve this. She would have done anything to avoid her upcoming torture. Anything. But these men had already taken everything. She had nothing with which to barter. And her mouth was gagged so that she could not beg or plead with the evil, enraged man. Her stomach tightened with anticipation of the pain to come.

The fury filled man looked long at his victim. Sweat was running down her luscious body, sweat from fear. Her belly undulated, making the fierce black bear head that was tattooed there seem to snarl back at him. Her eyes were as wide as saucers and tear filled, conveying her desperation. Her hands writhed in their confines and her pretty, naked breasts swayed and jerked as she twisted and turned to pull free. He decided that he wanted to hear her screams of agony as he pummeled her with the whip and so he stepped up to her and unfastened her gag from behind her head.

"Ohhhhhhhhhh!" the girl cried out when her lips were freed. "Pleeeeeease! Don't whip me, pleeeeeease! I'll do anything you want! Anything! Pleeeeeease!"

The sound of the girl's panicked cries was pleasing to the enraged crime boss. He pulled at her fear hardened nipples and twisted them until the girl moaned. Her feet did a little pitter patter on the floor as she tried to contain her frantic fear. Stepping away from her and to her side, the angry, hate filled killer reared his hand back and delivered a stinging blow with the long, thin whip across her pure, white breasts. The whip made a ringing noise as it passed through the air and a satisfying 'crack!' as it met her flesh.

"Ooooooooooo! Ooooooooooo! "Ooooooooooo!" the girl cried out. A bright red line had risen immediately along the path of the leather encased steel. He struck her again and again. Her screams became a howl and her face a mask of agony. She danced on her feet and tried to turn away from him. She only served to expose her long, smooth back to his attack.

'Crack!' A blow fell cross the sinewy tissue of her lower back. "Ahhhhhhhhhh! Ooooooooooo! Pleeeeeease!" the girl cried out. He struck it again and the girl twisted her body around only to receive a kiss of his whip across her upper thighs. "Plllllleeeeeease stop! Pleeeeeease!" she yelled.

Grobgy was relentless with his instrument of torture. Lines of red were forming all over her body, some of them dripping with thin trails of blood. The cruel gangster stood in one spot, letting the girl twist and turn to expose the unmarked parts of her body.

Outside Grobgy's office, two naked and trembling slave girls stood mesmerized by the sounds of agony coming through it. The door was thick and the sounds were muffled, and they both knew that inside the room the cries of torment had to be very loud to escape through it. They looked at each other and saw their own fear mirrored in each other's eyes. That could be them in there, and when the master was done, he might be looking for fresh meat. They quickly dashed away down the hall.

After a good fifteen minutes of relentless abuse, Yulia stopped struggling. Her beautiful body was crisscrossed with lacerations. Nothing in training had prepared her for this fierce beating. All of her energy was gone. Her body burned with the aftereffects of the blows. The man had whipped every part of her body that he could reach, up and down her thighs, across her breasts and belly. Even up and down her upraised arms. But the blows had stopped. Her head was hanging down and she slowly looked up to see whether her hellish Calvary was over. The man was panting from his exertions, the whip dangling from his right hand. He still had fire in his eyes though, and the girl moaned dismally.

Grobgy took in his handiwork. It had been a long time since he had really let go with a whip and it felt good. But another need was calling him now. His cock was as hard as the steel in the thin, pliant whip. He tossed the whip aside and pulled off his shirt. His chest was covered with a thick moss of black hair sprinkled with grey. Sweat made his skin glisten. He kicked off his boots and then unfastened his belt. When his pants were removed, he tossed them away from him and grabbed his cock. He needed to impale the unhappy, beautiful creature that he had just tormented.

Stepping behind the girl, he grabbed her by the hips. She groaned as his hands took possession of her tortured flesh. Her whole body shuddered. He took his hands and parted the torn, red lined, plump, rear mounds, revealing the girl's delicate, little, brown star. He presented his stiff pole to it and pressed it in.

Yulia had been well trained on how to open her rear portal for ravishment. She had learned to relax her muscles and arch her back to ease her possession. But she had no time to make herself ready for the man's assault and his thick cock tore her tender membranes as he invaded her. "Ohhhhhhhhh!" she cried out. "Ohhhhhhh!"

The fury inspired man groaned as he felt the tight ring of flesh grip his heated staff. The fact that the girl was moaning with pain and struggling to resist him made it all the better. When he had impaled himself within her to her depths, he reached around her torso and took hold of her battered breasts, squeezing them tightly. His hands reveled in the soft, resilient flesh as he compressed it. "Ahhhhhhh! Ahhhhhhh!" the girl cried out, dancing in her bonds.

The impassioned man didn't last long. He sawed his cock along the ring of flesh fervently. His juices began to rise almost immediately. When his cock began to throb and pulse within the girl's murky bowels, he roared his pleasure.

When his ejaculations ceased, the huge man slumped against the moaning body of his slave girl. All of his rage had left him. When he finally pulled back, he could feel his chest and thighs slick with sweat and the girl's blood. His palms were red. But his mind was tranquil. He bent over to the floor and recovered the girl's gag. She was still moaning and he muffled her miserable emanations by stuffing it back into her mouth. Dazed and exhausted from his exertions, he stepped over to a cabinet on the wall and took a slave hood out from it. He covered the poor girl's head and tightened it around her neck.

Yulia, the former Berkeley University undergraduate student, was actually grateful for the darkness which enveloped her. Her knees would not support her and she dangled in her chains, swaying slightly. She tried to rein in her desperate sobbing, but could not. What cruel fate had swept her into the hands of this madman, she thought miserably. How would she ever survive this hell to which she had been delivered? And all because she had rejected a lover, wanted to be free. She doubted that she could ever be less free than she was now. Her only consolation was that she could not live long if she was to be continuously maltreated like this. Her fevered, distraught mind welcomed the thought.

Covered with sweat and blood, Grobgy picked up his large, black leather chair from the floor and returned it to behind his desk. He slumped down into it. His eyes took in the form of the ravaged slave girl. He had gone a bit overboard, he realized. But that's what slave girls were for. He would send her down to the infirmary later where her lacerations would be washed and treated with salve. She was a pretty wench and had pleasured him well earlier. It wouldn't do to have her all scarred up.

His mind quickly let slip any thoughts of compassion for the girl and turned to the problem at hand. Who was fucking with him? He needed to find out as quickly as possible or he would be finished.

CHAPTER THREE
BEST INTENTIONS

About 250 kilometers northeast of where the unhappy slave girl, Yulia, hung virtually lifeless at the end of her chain, a tall, dark skinned ponygirl was being put through her paces. She, too, was no stranger to the whip. In fact, this morning, her dwarfish driver, Giorgi Gromyko, brother of Jerzy, Lightning's driver, had given her ten strokes on her breasts and belly. Jackie, now known as Chocolate, didn't know why. Or rather, she knew why, but didn't know if there was anything particular that she had done or not done that had precipitated the onslaught of the riding crop. Why she was beaten was because she was a ponygirl and her driver was a cruel, ruthless, ponygirl driver intent on demonstrating his power over her at every opportunity.

They were running on the estate's practice track. Chocolate didn't know why she was running there rather than over at the main track where the races were held. All she knew was that this morning she had been given another reason to obey her driver's commands without question and that she intended not to give him another excuse for beating her now. She had been running all morning, starts and stops, long, fast intervals and then slow ones. Right now she was on an endurance run, ten times around the track. Her driver was keeping her at a medium pace, but was keenly perceptive about any slacking off from steady, double time strides. Three times his whip had struck her cruelly on her naked rump, sending an intense message of pain to her. She had shaken off her weariness and resumed her stride.

Two men were standing by the rail near the home turn watching Chocolate's performance with interest. The first one, about 50, was tall and broad shouldered. He was well dressed in smart but casual clothes, a green and black checkered, short sleeved, Italian knit shirt and finely creased dark brown slacks. His shoes, which had become obscured with the dust of the training area, were of finely tooled, black leather and had been spit shined earlier that morning by a dutiful, obedient, pretty slave girl.

The other was a slender but well fit man, about 5'6" tall. He was in his mid-thirties and dressed in jeans and a dark blue t-shirt that stretched over his well formed chest. He wore very practical brown work boots. He was smoking a Lucky Strike cigarette and from time to time blew a grayish cloud over the track. His face was lean and intent. Both men were taking in Chocolate's training session with more than academic interest.

"Well, she looks pretty good to me," the tall man said to the other. This was Michael Burnham, the American billionaire that everyone was talking about. The other, smaller man was Jake Barnes, his 'fixer' and co-conspirator in the long pending rescue of Burnham's niece, Maddy, now known as Lightning.

Jake had been the one to locate Maddy after her kidnapping. He and his crew had traced her to Kalikastan through a slaving operation in Elizabeth, New Jersey. But they did not know where she had been taken or how to get into the insular country. It had been Jake's idea to take over the slaving operation and establish a working criminal relationship with the men at the other end. Burnham used his vast wealth to practically buy his way into ownership of an estate in the Kalikastani hinterland. Burnham's company became top bidder on a huge pipeline project going through the country sponsored by a consortium of Western European countries. The tradeoff for the Russian gangsters that ran the country was being allowed to belly up to the trough of corruption that was being siphoned off. There were millions to be made by everybody and the ruling National Commission had made Burnham an honorary citizen.

The problem was, at least as far as Jake saw it, was that Burnham had become completely enamored of the Kalikastani way of doing things. While at first he was reticent to involve himself too deeply in the culture of female slavery, he had since then gone native, so to speak. He now owned a full stable of racing ponies and a large staff of beautiful, compliant slave girls to go with it. He had moved his corporate operations center here and even enslaved his former secretary, Libby. Burnham was a real go getter and not only had initiated his own slave girl training center, he had also cemented an alliance with the underworlds of the US, China and Southeast Asia to facilitate the exchange of heroin, stolen technology, pirated goods and, of course, enslaved, young females.

Jake had wanted to put together an operation to snatch Maddy from Grobgy, but Burnham had nixed it. He didn't want to upset his applecart of corruption and pleasure he had established here. So Jake came up with another idea. He had recruited the beautiful African American call girl, Jackie, with a promise of a cash payment of one million dollars, to volunteer to be kidnapped and brought to Burnham's estate where she would be turned into a ponygirl. Burnham would arrange a match race between

Jackie, now known as Chocolate because of her delicious, smooth dark skin, and Maddy, now known as Lightning.

The idea was that Jackie, who was a track star in Chicago before she became a hooker, would compete in the 1500 meter sulky, win a berth in the fall championships and meet and beat Lightning in the finals. But something had gone wrong. They had registered the new pony in the 1500 only to find out that Lightning was running the 3000 meter this season. And so it was back to the drawing board.

But Jake had another brain storm. If Chocolate could champion in the 1500, they could still challenge Grobgy to a claiming race once the season was over. It was believed that Grobgy would not be able to refuse the race for fear of losing face in the racing establishment. But the key was that Chocolate had to win the championship, since otherwise Grobgy would have no reason to accept a challenge from a clearly inferior pony.

So far everything was going okay. While Chocolate had hit some bumps in the road in her early training, she had proved to be a real competitor and now had won all her races but one. If she continued on this pace, she was a shoe in for the fall tournament and virtually a sure thing to champion. Lightning was on a winning streak too and it seemed that she would certainly make the tournament. But she had to win the 3000 meter championship for everything to work out. If she failed, there would be no sense to the match race.

The key to the strategy was to secretly train Chocolate to run the 3000 meter while, at the same time, keeping her in shape to win the 1500. That's why she was here now on the estate practice track away from the public's prying eyes. All the other ponies were over at the magnificently refurbished main track showing off for the benefit of the hoi polloi. Chocolate was spending another day hard at work.

Jake watched Chocolate complete another lap. He had been told by her trainer, Irkut, an old timer as far as ponyracing was concerned and coaxed out of retirement by Burnham's money, not to show himself to the pony. While Irkut had been told that she had been specially recruited by Jake as a ringer, he didn't know that she was a shill to accomplish the rescue of Burnham's niece.

The fact that Lightning was Burnham's niece was a closely guarded secret. Jake and Burnham and all of Jake's boys would be pushing up Kalikastani daisies if the National Commission ever found out. And so Irkut was kept in the dark and allowed to believe that Jake had actually kidnapped Jackie against her will. Jake had let it slip that he knew Jackie from her call girl days and Irkut had strongly recommended that Jake stay out of sight whenever Chocolate was around. It was generally held that ponygirls should not have any reminders of their prior human state, especially in their first few years. Ponygirl training depended heavily on the acceptance by the pony of its permanent new station in life. If a pony had any thought that it could be rescued, it lost some of its motivation to mindless obedience.

But today, Jake had received a pass from Irkut to watch Chocolate run. Giorgi was running her with her blinders down, two Velcro tabs that sat above the little eye holes on the ponygirl hoods. It was used whenever it was thought that it was advisable or desirable to deprive a pony of its sight. Oftentimes, ponies were made to train with their tabs down. Ponies needed to be instantly responsive to the direction they received through their reins.

Complete and full obedience was needed during a race. A driver might, for his own reasons, want a pony to run the outside, or try to slip by on the inside rail. He might want her to shift to the right or left to block a surging opponent, or hold back its speed deceptively until the final push to victory. If a pony believed that it could rely on its own vision and will to make these kinds of judgments, the whole strategy of a race could be lost. And so, they were oftentimes run in training completely blinded, depending only on the wisdom and skill of their driver to prevent them from running into a rail.

Jake tossed his butt away and released the last cloud of smoke from his lungs before responding to his boss. Jackie looked good all right. But Jake was suffering from a crisis of conscience. Jackie had trusted him without knowing the full extent of what it would be like to be a ponygirl. He had told her all about it, but you really had to see it to believe it. And her driver was notoriously cruel.

Jake was no schoolboy. He had done some pretty nasty things in his trade. But he had never broken his word. He had promised Jackie that she would be freed after the racing season was over, win or lose. But he was beginning to believe that Burnham would renege on the deal. He was too much into it. His soul had been corrupted. Would the billionaire voluntarily give up ownership of a champion ponygirl? He had begun to doubt it. Burnham had surrounded himself with Russian gangsters who acted as his security now. Jake had been pushed to the sidelines. But he was determined to keep his pledge to Jackie, by hook or by crook, that is, if Burnham's Russian goons didn't kill him first.

"Yeah, she looks good all right, Mr. Burnham," Jake replied. In fact, she looked damn good. She had always been a looker, with large, sensuous, well formed breasts, long, muscular legs, and enticing, curvaceous body. But three months of ponygirl training had made her even more alluring, trimmed out the plump rear cheeks, worked off the tiny role of fat that she had started to grow on her enticing hips, gave her the muscular, well formed thighs of a mare.

Jake had been an occasional customer of the 22 year old former whore. He had helped her out of a real tight spot once and she always threw him an enthusiastic, free fuck when he was in the mood. It was partly her feeling of obligation to him that had, he was sure, convinced her to agree to the plan. That was just one more reason to keep his word. But he wouldn't mind fucking her again now. He had visited her one night in the ponybarn when she had been affixed to the rail in her stall and unable to turn to see who was plowing her welcoming cunt. But since racing season had started she was off limits. Well, there were slave girls aplenty to sate his needs and he would seek one as soon as this tete te with Burnham was done.

"Has Grobgy bit at the bait yet?" he asked his boss after a pause to watch Chocolate's heavy breasts swaying and jerking as she passed by.

"Not yet, but I know that he's interested," Burnham replied. Grobgy was interested for a reason that Burnham had not disclosed to his increasingly inconvenient employee. He had told Jake that the deal would be that if Chocolate won, they would get Maddy and somehow, by faking her and Chocolate's deaths, sneak them out of the country. But, he had told Jake that if Lightning won, he would give Grobgy a big slice of the corruption from the pipeline. Burnham had proposed no such thing. He knew that, as a sportsman, money would not be an inducement for Grobgy to put Lightning up in a claiming race. He had already tried to buy her directly and had been told clearly and emphatically that the pony was not for sale at any price. No, the only carrot that would entice the gangster and ponygirl devotee was the possibility of owning both the 1500 and 3000 meter champions. So if Chocolate lost, she would become Grobgy's and remain a ponygirl for the rest of her useful days.

Burnham knew that Jake would kill him if he found out. He wanted to send Jake and his boys home, but Jake would smell a rat right away. He could have him and his boys taken for a ride, Russian style, but that would raise too many questions from the powers that be. And, in fact, he still needed Jake as a counterweight to the Russians. He was not absolutely sure of the loyalty of his Russian henchmen and Jake and his hard bitten, experienced men were a kind of insurance policy. He knew he would have to deal with Jake at some point. But that was then and this was now. For the time being, he would keep the efficient fixer and killer close.

Chocolate had finished her tenth lap around the 1500 meter track and was coasting along at a cool down pace. It took a while for her breath to return to a comfortable, slower rhythm. Having been blinded, she didn't know how far she had run, but she knew it had been a long time, much further than her racing distance. Her eyes were open under her hood, there being a small space between them and the fabric, and it was as if the light had gone out all over the world. Her eyes peered into nothingness. But the absence of visual stimulation made her more conscious of her body and its reactions to her workout. She could feel it steeped with sweat. Her legs were tired and bereft of energy. But they felt good. Her whole physical being was effused with the warmth of her expenditures. When her driver really got her going, she felt like she could run forever.

The dark skinned pony dutifully put one foot in front of the other as she obeyed the command of her reins. Life as a ponygirl wasn't all that bad. Once she had gotten over her rebellion at being dehumanized, tortured and confined, had come to accept that resistance was futile, Jackie had let herself become immersed in her new role. Some of the men were mean and callous, but so were some of the men she had serviced as a high priced whore back in Chicago. Her driver was ruthless and controlled her with a will of iron, but he fucked her several times a day and had his blond haired slave girl service her frequently. Her body had never been in such great shape. It was full of energy and was taut and solid. The running was exhilarating, even when she was worked hard like today.

But it was the racing that was the best. Jackie hated to lose, even when she had run track back in high school. Once she had gotten over the strange experience of being presented naked and trussed like an animal before the roaring crowds, she had begun to revel in their enthusiasm for her. On race day, her body would reverberate with excitement and anticipation of her event. Her driver never allowed her release on race day until she had run her race and then only if she had won. But she won almost all of her events and pranced back to the pony camp eagerly, a wreath of flowers circling her neck, knowing that she would get a satisfying, prolonged, carnal reward.

Giorgi stopped the cart right in front of where Burnham and Jake were standing. Jake watched the diminutive man jump off and bring a plastic bottle of water to the pony's lips. He admired her slick, sweat covered body. She wore the snarling, black dog's head that was Burnham's estate insignia tattooed on her hard, trim belly, and her name, in bright blue, Cyrillic letters stenciled on her chest.

While he had, at first, been shocked at the dehumanized state of the ponygirls, during the many months that he had spent in Kalikastan he had grown to appreciate the intense sexual thrill he received when near them. The trainers and drivers treated them just like animals, never talking to them beyond a few short, curt commands necessary for their duties. Their faces were never seen. It was easy to begin to think of them as other than women. As he looked at the naked, beautiful body of the brown skinned ponygirl, her humanity obscured by her clinging, tight hood, he had to remind himself that Jackie was in there and not some strange, new form of being.

Chocolate's large, round breasts shivered deliciously as her chest rose and fell. Her hairless slit beckoned him. Jake watched as the driver took the ample mounds in his small, strong hands and began to caress them. The pony's body seemed to melt under his attentions. The small man kissed and sucked at her teats while stroking the appealing, hairless slit between her thighs. Jake watched as the tiny fingers slid inside, spreading her moisture and causing the pony to moan.

Giorgi stepped back and uttered a sharp command in Russian to the enflamed pony. She immediately sank to her knees, planting them in the dusty surface of the track. He reached behind her hooded head and released the straps that held her leather encased, steel bit between her teeth. Chocolate stretched her liberated mouth and tongue and then, at another command, lowered her torso so that her head was level with the small man's loins and spread her plump lips into an 'O'. Giorgi had freed his hardened cock from his pants and, after taking hold of the long, brown ponytail that sprung from the back of the pony's hood, thrust it home.

Jake watched, entranced, as Chocolate's mouth and lips worked the man's tool. It was amazing to him that the dwarf's cock was man sized and it seemed slightly grotesque when compared to his diminutive frame. His own cock was rock hard as he imagined that it was his piece sliding back and forth into the brown skinned pony's mouth, taking in the exquisite sensations of the moist warmth and the agile tongue.

Chocolate's breasts swung freely beneath her chest as she was rocked back and forth by the dwarf's hand in her hair. Her own hands, bound and useless behind her, were clasped into fists. She was still bound in her traces and the leather reins that were hooked to her harness and the two long poles connected to her hips ran back behind her to the cart. Although Jake could not see the pony's face, her grunts and moans as she consumed the large, thick wand of flesh seemed to signal her enjoyment of the opportunity to pleasure her driver.

In fact, Jackie was enjoying the feel of the man's hot cock in her mouth. Her passions had been ignited by the man's caresses. While she had always been passionate, her lusts seemed to be lying always now just below the surface and all it took was a stroke of her breasts or a caress of her cunt to make her begin to moisten. Although she was still blinded, something told her that someone was watching, a kind of sixth sense, and the idea that she could display her skills, make whoever was witnessing her pleasuring of her master's cock desire her, was exciting. And she knew that soon her driver, or his pretty slave girl, would satisfy her own lustful needs.

The little man did not take long to stiffen and grunt as he poured his essence into the pony's obedient mouth. Jake watched as his eyes rolled back and his body sagged. Chocolate's grunts rose in volume as she drank down every drop of his spewm. The man gave her mouth one, long hard, last thrust, pausing to let it finish its throbbing deep in the pony's throat.

Giorgi did not say anything to the Americans after he pulled his prick from the pony's compliant lips. He reattached her bit and ordered her to her feet. He hated the Americans. But he welcomed the chance to beat his brother, Jerzy, when the two ponies finally met in the claiming race at the end of the season. The opportunity to best him, and the sizable monetary inducement as well, had been the reasons he had agreed to race for these foreigners. That and the prospect of another championship season. But he didn't have anything but contempt for the interlopers. He had wanted to flaunt his control over the American billionaire's property and that was why he had used her in front of them. During the season, the voluptuous animal was his and his alone. They could eat their hearts out.

Jake and Burnham watched as the small man hopped back up to the cart and snapped the reins. Chocolate started off immediately into a slow trot, on her way back to the pony camp.

* * * * * * * * * * * * * *

Two other men had been watching Chocolate run, standing down on the track just after the home turn. One, a small, lanky man wearing a pair of crisp, newly minted blue jeans and a white, short sleeve, poplin shirt was Irving Ostroff. He was one of Jake's guys. But he wasn't one of the heavies. Irving was Jake's techie. He ran his own independent lab back in the States and was called in from time to time to help Jake out whenever he needed a gadget or some forensic work done. It was Irving who had unearthed the clues that had enabled them to discover what had happened to Maddy. He was a nerdish type, with thick, black framed glasses and a school boy mien. All that was missing was the plastic pocket protector. But Irving got the job done and knew full well that Jake's work required discretion at the highest level.

Irving had been flown in from the States a couple of weeks ago to take a look at the standard sulky cart that Chocolate was pulling and to determine if he could improve on the design within the limits of racing regulations. Chocolate would need every edge that she could get to beat Lightning. Irving had made a number of suggestions. First, he proposed moving the driver's seat from the center of the cart to slightly to the left side. This would reduce centrifugal force as she made her turns. Second, he had proposed using a special alloy on the frame to lighten it. And then there was the special lubricant he had created, tilting the wheels slightly for better traction and some others.

The reason Irving was on the track was so that he could videotape the cart's performance in real conditions. He had finished putting it together after the parts had been flown in from his lab in the States. He would examine the footage carefully when Chocolate was done running for the day and make any adjustments that he thought necessary. The cart would not debut until the fall tournament.

The man standing next to Irving was Irkut, Chocolate's trainer. Irkut was a traditionalist when it came to ponygirl racing. He had protested when he was told of the development of the new cart. But he had gone over the design carefully and had confirmed that it met all of the racing regulations. He had been dubious that it would improve the pony's performance, but as he had watched Chocolate make her rounds, he had been impressed. Tomorrow, when the cart had been fine tuned, they would do actual time trials. But his expert eyes had seen enough to convince him that he was watching a revolution in the sport.

Irkut was not a voluble man, but his excitement was tangible. "That's one fucking fine cart, Amerikanski," he told the scientist. "She runs real good."

Irving took his eye from the viewfinder of the tripod mounted camera. "I know," Irving replied. "I'll bet it takes at least ten seconds off of her best time tomorrow." Irving was a proud professional. He found the whole concept of ponygirl racing and female slavery distasteful to say the least. But he had been given a job and he would do it to perfection. And he had another motive besides his professionalism.

Many months ago, when Jake and his men had uncovered the Georgia farm where Maddy had first been held prisoner, they had discovered a woman locked in a cage in a hidden cellar underneath the barn. Jake had wanted to leave her there. They had just watched three other young women hauled off to slavery in a laundry van, a van which they had ultimately traced to the warehouse in

Elizabeth. Jake's position was that they had one goal and one goal only: find and rescue Maddy. What happened to other women was none of their concern. If the woman in the cellar was rescued, what would they do with her? If she was freed and sent home, it would blow the whole investigation and Maddy's kidnappers might go to ground, never to be found. And they couldn't hold the woman prisoner themselves.

But Irving had been adamant. And so Jake had brought the heavyset, not what you would call attractive, Maureen to the surface. Irving had washed and cleaned her and found her some clothes. He felt pity for the sizable, forlorn, young woman and promised her that she would be taken care of. Jake had proposed that she be held incognito in some private mental hospital for the duration and Irving had, against his better judgment, agreed.

Burnham was supposed to arrange it. But the billionaire had instead arranged for Maureen to be disposed of. He didn't give a shit about her and didn't want her possible sudden appearance to gum up the works. The FBI would be all over them. Burnham had thought that the men he had hired to get rid of her would find a convenient place to dig a little, or in Maureen's case, a big hole and dump her in it. But, under the principle of waste not want not, the men had sold her off to slavers in Mexico. Maureen had spent the past months as an inmate in a whorehouse in southern Mexico catering to the more exquisite tastes of the local high society.

Irving had been after Jake ever since Maureen had been taken away to disclose where she was being held. When Jake had failed to give him a satisfactory answer, Irving had begun to suspect that Maureen had suffered a cruel fate.

When Jake had called him to fly to Kalikastan to do his magic on the sulky cart, Irving had seen his opportunity. He had left behind with a confidential source the whole story about the slaving operation, Maureen's disappearance, Burnham's role in it, everything. If he didn't call that certain someone everyday, the package would be released to the New York Times, the Washington Post and the FBI. Irving knew that the release of the information would be his own death warrant, but he didn't care. He needed to know what happened to Maureen and he was willing to risk his life on it.

Burnham was apoplectic when he realized that he was being blackmailed. As far as he knew, Maureen was pushing up daisies somewhere. He blessed his luck when he found out that she was still alive. He immediately made arrangements for her recovery. Irving had insisted that she be produced in the flesh so that he could be sure that she was alive and not be fooled by some trick. Jake had told him that Maureen would arrive later today by helicopter.

Irving closed up his equipment and strode off of the dirt track. He saw Burnham and Jake watching him, but he had nothing to say to them. As far as he was concerned, the sooner that he finished his job here and was able to bring Maureen home with him the better. He would watch the videos on his laptop in his room back at the mansion. He had designed a special program that would help him analyze it. Tomorrow he would make the final adjustments.

As Irving crossed through the gate in the fence surrounding the track a naked, brown haired slave girl rose from her knees and began to follow him back to the mansion. Irving's stride was firm and determined and she had to scurry to keep up with him. God help her if she let him get away from her, especially with her master and owner watching.

The scrawny scientist had left Burnham's office two weeks ago after he had made his deal for the liberation of Maureen and had been escorted to his room on the third floor of the luxurious mansion by one of Burnham's Russian guards. He had known about the slaving operation and knew that he would see slave girls here, but he was unprepared for the reality of it. It was offensive to everything that he believed. There had even been a naked, forlorn woman in a cage in Burnham's office. And the ponygirls! Their existence defied belief. How could men do such a thing and live with themselves? His heart had cried out for them when he saw them trundling along the track outside, hooded, naked and bound, their driver's cracking whips to make them run faster. What could their life be like?

Irving had promised himself that he would have nothing to do with the callous exploitation of the slave girls and certainly not with the ponygirls while he was in Kalikastan. His conscience was already bothered enough by the role he had played in making the takeover of the Elizabeth slaving operation possible. He tried to ignore the beautiful, naked bodies as he passed through the mansion, hurrying past him to some assignment or standing obediently silent and still while they awaited their next ravishment.

When he entered his large, high ceiling, finely appointed room, he was prepared to open his laptop and begin some sketches for the new ponygirl cart. But there, kneeling on the large, four poster bed, was a naked, pale, black haired girl. She looked up at him expectantly as he entered.

"What are you doing here?" he asked her curtly. She had fine, round breasts and deliciously curvaceous hips. Her lips were full and pouting and her dark eyes were outlined prettily. On her belly, just above her dainty, hairless slit, was tattooed the large, rabid looking dog's head that was the symbol of Burnham's estate. On her chest, over her breasts, her name was stenciled in Russian. She wore a thick, leather collar around her neck and leather bracelets on her wrists and ankles.

The girl looked back at him, apparently put off by his brusque question. She seemed to be searching for a proper way to answer him.

Irving put down his suitcase and laptop. "I said, 'What are you doing here?'" he repeated angrily.

A look of fright crossed the girl's lovely face. It took her another moment to marshal a response.

"M,may I serve you, master?" she uttered in a low, plaintive voice. She had a heavy accent, Rumanian or Bulgarian, thought Irving. He guessed correctly that she didn't have enough English to understand the question. He waived his hand at her, beckoning her to approach him. Her eyes lit up and she crawled across the bed and then padded over to him on her bare feet. Her breasts swayed delightfully as she moved towards him.

Irving took hold of her arm and escorted her to the door. "Tell Mr. Burnham, 'Thanks, but no thanks,'" he told her. He opened the door and pushed her out of the room. She looked up at him forlornly, tears forming in her eyes. "P,please, may I serve you, master," she said again, her voice a little more urgent.

"No!" Irving shouted and he slammed the door behind her.

The scientist spent the next few hours going over some designs. There was a finely carved, polished, dark oak desk in the room and he sat at it while he worked. The desk was set in front of a large set of windows and whenever he looked out he could see the ponygirls running their laps outside on the track below. He tried to ignore them, just as he tried to ignore the array of whips and chains that were mounted on the walls. He would have no use for them.

After an hour or so, he decided that he needed some refreshment and he picked up the telephone that sat on the desk and asked that a pot of coffee and a sandwich be sent up to his room. After about twenty minutes there was a light tapping at the door. He got up and, crossing the room, opened it. There, in the hallway, was the small, black haired girl holding a tray with his coffee and sandwich on it. Her hands were trembling, making the plate and coffee cup on the tray jingle slightly. He opened the door wider so that she could come in. He wondered what could make the girl so afraid of serving him. But when she passed him to place the tray on the desk, he saw several long, fresh whip marks on her back.

"What happened to you?" he exclaimed. And then he realized how stupid his question was. Someone had whipped the girl in the last hour since she had left his room. He couldn't imagine what this obsequious, timid girl could have done to warrant such savage treatment.

The girl put the tray down at the desk and looked at him forlornly. Tears had formed in her eyes. Her lips were trembling as she spoke again the only words he had heard her say, "May I please you master?" This time there was a distinct tone of desperation in her voice.

Irving's heart went out to the poor slave girl. He wondered what kind of life she had been stolen from, how long she had been forced to serve the whims of her callous masters. She was so young, barely twenty he guessed. She stood only a little over five feet tall. She was thin, but her breasts were ample, invitingly ample. His eyes fixed on them for a moment and he wondered what it would be like to caress them. Despite his horror and revulsion at her forced subservience, he felt his loins stir.

The principled scientist shook off his reverie and spoke to the girl in a caring, gentle voice. "Don't worry, no one's going to whip you here. I'm not going to hurt you." He took his hand and stroked the side of her head in a gesture of comfort. The girl's eyes lit up for a moment.

"May I please you, master," she repeated, the beginnings of a smile on her face.

"No, no, no," Irving returned in a soothing voice. "You don't have to do that. Now, why don't you go back to the kitchen or wherever they sent you from and try to keep out of trouble."

He grabbed her arm and started to escort her to the door once again. The girl gave a sob and the tears started to flow down her face. Irving patted her head. "That's all right, you'll be okay. I won't tell anyone you were crying."

He opened the door and guided her out. "Come back later and you can take my plate and coffee cup back to the kitchen, okay?"

Irving closed the door again and went back to his desk. He had ordered a chicken salad sandwich and it was fresh and delicious. It had been served on thick, moist, black bread with a generous dollop of mayonnaise and slices of rich, red tomato. The coffee was fresh too and had a heavy, robust flavor to it. He finished the sandwich quickly and got back to work.

Outside, it had begun to get dark. He watched as some of the ponygirls were escorted back to the barn. He wondered what kinds of cruelty they would be subject to in there. He could just imagine what treatment they received from the evil men who treated them like animals. What could life possibly be like for them? He felt a pang of guilt that he was aiding Burnham in his nefarious hobby, even if it was in the interests of saving Maddy and recovering Maureen from whatever hell she had been sent to. Maybe he would go to the authorities anyway once he and Maureen were safely back in the States. It would be his death warrant, he knew that. But how could he live with the thought that he could have done something to free all of these women, hundreds of them, maybe thousands from what he could tell, but instead had done nothing, let them spend the remainder of their lives as sexual chattel.

He had completed the first set of drawing and specifications. They had not given him an Internet connection and he needed to get these files back to his lab in Florida as soon as possible. He downloaded them to his jump drive and got up from the desk. He was stretching his arms and yawning when there was another tap on his door. He guessed it was the black haired slave girl coming back for his dishes. He walked to the door and opened it.

It was the little slave girl all right. She gave him a supplicative look. Her eyes were wet with tears and she was shaking. But what he noticed mostly were the angry red stripes all over her tender breasts. Somebody had really gone to town on her. Bright red lines criss-crossed them like a thatch work.

"Oh my God!" Irving exclaimed. He took her by the arm and pulled her into the room. When he shut the door the girl dropped to her knees and started to sob. She bent over and took hold of his foot, kissing and licking it. "Please, please, may I serve you, master, please?" she begged forlornly. "Please, may Marika serve you master, please?"

And then it struck him. Now he realized why she had been beaten. She had been whipped because he had sent her away. The irony of the fact that he had done her harm while trying to spare her struck him like a fist. What kind of surreal world was he in, he thought. She had been punished because he had declined to rape her. For there was no doubt in his mind that it was rape. She had no more power to consent to her sexual use than she had to refuse. And unconsented to sexual acts were rape!

Irving leaned over and, taking the girl by her shoulders, brought her torso up from the floor. "There, there, now," he said soothingly, "I won't send you away. Don't cry. I understand. You can stay."

A flash of hope crossed the girl's pretty, tear stained face. "Marika may serve you?" she asked timidly.

"Yes, yes," he answered. "You can serve me. Okay?"

The girl's eyes brightened. She reached her hands out for Irving's fly and started to pull it down. The startled scientist pushed her hands away.

"No, no, not that," he said nervously. "You don't have to do that. It's okay."

The girl frowned and then made a gesture towards the bed. "Master will fuck Marika?" she asked hopefully.

"No, master will not fuck Marika," he replied. "I told you that you didn't have to do that. You can stay here for now. Okay?"

Marika looked at him confused. And then her gaze went to the wall full of whips and other implements of torture. "M,master will whip Marika?" she asked unhappily.

Irving was getting exasperated. "No!" he shouted. "I'm not going to hurt you!" He saw a cloud pass over the girl's face at his outburst. Frustrated, Irving pointed to the bed. "Get up there," he ordered.

Marika sprang to her feet and rushed over to the large, comfortable bed. She quickly and expertly pulled down the covers and jumped up on it. She turned her back on Irving and bent over on her knees, spreading her thighs widely. Her delicate, soft, shaven labial lips peaked out from beneath her, the little golden disks that denoted her ownership dangling from them. Her rear cheeks were sooth and soft. She made a delectable sight. For a moment, Irving wondered what it would be like to fuck her. It was what everyone expected, apparently even the girl. She was undoubtedly highly trained in the arts of physical love. She had probably been raped a hundred times or more already.

The principled tech guy pulled his speculations short. "No!" he thought to himself. "I won't do it. It's wrong. I won't add to this girl's misery. She can stay, but I won't rape her. Even if she begs me."

He remembered his jump drive and the need to get his files emailed to the States. He knew that someone would have an Internet connection somewhere. He decided to leave the girl to her own devices. He would deal with her later.

It took Irving an hour to find someone who could help him. Burnham had converted one wing of the mansion to offices and a lanky young man dressed in a white shirt and tie took the jump drive from him. Irving was shocked when he realized that he was an American.

"Yeah, no problem," the youth said. He looked like he was about 25 or 26. He had that self confident, arrogant insouciance that Americans abroad were known for. He was sitting behind a large computer desk formed into an el. A blond haired slave girl knelt in the corner of the room, her hands locked behind her head, her thighs spread widely. She had small, conical breasts with long, thin nipples. On her belly was tattooed a bright green, coiled snake, venom dripping from its sharp, exposed fangs. She was thin and pale, but she had enough meat on her to make her form seem languorous. She smiled uncertainly at him when he looked at her.

"I've got to get the contents cleared first," the young man told him. "Mr. Burnham has to okay all outside communications. He's out now, but I believe that he'll be back early tomorrow afternoon."

"This can't wait until tomorrow afternoon," Irving told him, exasperated. "I've got to get the prototypes made as soon as possible."

"Sorry, Mr. Ostroff," the kid replied. "Orders are orders."

"What's your name?" Irving asked him demandingly. "I want to know to tell Mr. Burnham that who fucked up this project."

The young man looked back at him unconcernedly. "You can tell him that Bruce Jenkins obeyed his most important standing order rather than get dumped in a shallow grave somewhere. Okay?"

Irving realized that arguing was going to get him nowhere. He would have to speak to Burnham tomorrow about getting his own Internet connection. Otherwise, this project was going to take weeks.

The cavernous hallways of the luxurious residence/corporate headquarters were filled with scurrying, naked slave girls, armed Russian gangsters and neatly dressed American corporate types. All of them seemed accepting of the strange life that they were living. Here and there, pretty, young girls were shackled to rings in the walls or kneeling expectantly gagged and with their arms bound behind them waiting for their next assignment.

Irving, not wanting to go back to his room and face the dilemma of what to do with the pretty, black haired slave girl there, took his time wandering around the mansion. He found his way to the lounge only to walk back out of it quickly when he saw the patrons engaging in various forms of sexual union there. There was a large garden behind the building, full of brilliant flowers and carefully manicured topiary. But even there he came across a slave girl on her knees servicing one of the black t-shirted Russians in one of the alcoves.

He finally decided that he had avoided the issue long enough and made his way back to the third floor. He had decided that the girl could stay in his room as long as she wanted, but that he would not succumb to her charms. He had made a pledge not to exploit any of the enslaved women while he was in Kalikastan and he was determined to keep it.

When Irving came back into his room, he saw the girl still kneeling on his bed. She was in the exact pose as he had left her, bent over with her forehead on the pillow, her legs spread wide. She didn't even flinch at the sound of the door opening and closing.

It was early evening in Kalikastan, but he had had a thirteen hour flight that had started at seven at night in Miami. He was tired from all the traveling, tired from the stress of his confrontation with Burnham, tired of wrestling with his conscience. He decided that he would take a shower and go to bed. Tomorrow was another day and he would work some more on the designs for the new racing cart.

There was a spacious, beautifully designed bathroom appurtenant to his room and Irving went into it. The walls were covered with rose colored tiles and a deep pile, dark red rug on the floor. The faucets and other plumbing appointments were gold plated down to the handle on the toilet. The towel racks were made of a finely polished, dark oak. It was the most luxurious bathroom he had ever been in. And this was just a guest room. He wondered what luxury Burnham immersed himself in and how much of it was paid for by his trade in human flesh. Probably not much, since Burnham had been obscenely wealthy before he even came here and he was, as Jake had told him, pulling down millions from the pipeline project. Well, he thought, it was no concern of his. He was not the policeman of the world. He would help save Maddy, save Maureen and get out as quickly as he could.

The shower was set in a corner and surrounded on two sides by walls of smoky, etched glass, with designs of various giant, blooming flowers on it. He quickly disrobed and stepped in. There was room enough for three people in it and it had, aside from the showerhead, outlets for sprays that could emanate from the tiled walls to immerse the occupant in a cascade of water. In one of the walls was a series of shelves that contained a wide variety of designer shampoos, rinses, soaps and body washes. Irving was a plain guy and he selected a bar of what looked like the simplest soap there before he turned on the water.

He luxuriated in the shower for a long time. The flow from the showerhead was hot and strong and it sent a relaxing message to his tired body. He found his mind wandering to the many examples of female pulchritude he had seen that day, more beautiful, young women than he had ever seen in one place before. The picture of the naked brown haired girl he had seen on her knees in the garden sprung into his head. He had not seen her face, but her torso was long and slender, her ass a perfect, smooth plumpness. The man's hands had been resting lightly on her head and his eyes had been rolled back, his mouth open, as he enjoyed her service to his prick.

Unconsciously, Irving's hand strayed to his loins. He began to stroke his cock idly as he imagined what an expert, willing mouth would feel like right now. His manhood had become fully erect before he realized what he was doing. He quickly released himself and shook himself out of his reverie. He would have to keep things like that out of his mind if he was going to maintain his resolve. He grabbed a bottle of shampoo and while he washed and rinsed his hair, he tried to concentrate on algorithms and other algebraic formulas. His hair was short and he was able to complete the tasks of washing and rinsing it quickly. When done, he turned off the water and stepped out of the shower to dry himself.

The towel was large and soft and of fine, absorbent quality. He rubbed his body down quickly and then donned the fluffy, terrycloth bathrobe that was hanging on a hook for his convenience. When he opened the door to the bathroom, the first thing that he saw was the pale, soft body of the slave girl, right where he had left her. Her black hair was shrouding her face, but she had her braceleted hands behind her back and he could see the side of her right breast crushed against her knee. Her bare thighs were slender and graceful. Her pale skin was unblemished but for the angry red stripes on her back that he had inadvertently helped put there. She was a temptation all right. Too much of one to share a bed with him.

He decided that he would tell her that she could sleep on the floor. There was an extra blanket on the bed that he would not need and plenty of pillows. He crawled up on the bed and placed his hand on her back to shake her from the spell that he had seemed to have placed her in when he ordered her up on the bed earlier. The girl's skin was smooth and warm. He shook her lightly and she stirred, rising from her bent over position to her knees. Her soft, round breasts swayed slightly as she rose. He noticed that her nipples were fat and succulent. She turned to look at him expectantly. Her lips were moist and plump and her face was pleasing. As she opened her mouth, he knew what she was going to say before she said it.

"May Marika please you, master?" she asked. Her voice was low and husky. Her tongue slipped out between her lips and washed them. She arched her back, making her breasts jut out and she swayed her torso slightly, making them stir. She had brought her small, delicate hands from behind her back and she placed one of them on Irving's thigh. His robe had slid open and his leg was exposed up to his hip. Irving's reply caught in his throat as the hand gently ascended his leg until it reached the crux of his thigh and his hip and then slid down again.

Irving felt his cock hardening. He was spellbound by the girl's beauty and sensuousness. She must have sensed that she was gaining the upper hand, so to speak, since she edged herself a little closer to him so that her bare breasts were inches away from his chest. She placed her other hand on his arm and burrowed her head between his neck and his shoulder, brushing her lips along his neck. Irving caught a whiff of an earthy, entrancing perfume. He had not been so close to her before and he hadn't noticed it. It did something to him, reminding him of all the beautiful, unattainable women he had ever seen in his life. This girl was beautiful too. But she wasn't unattainable. In fact, she was very much the opposite. He didn't need any of the debonair, suave pick up lines that he could never think of at the time. He didn't have to worry that his nerdish appearance would make the woman laugh at his presumptuous advance. She would not, could not, say no.

Irving felt his resolution wavering. He was just about to push her away when the hand on his thigh slid surreptitiously a little higher and to the right and the experienced fingers surrounded his hardened manhood. It was his sigh that betrayed him. The sound of it in his own ears drowned out his mental protestations. The girl had heard it too and knew that it signaled victory for her long, relentless campaign to seduce him. Her head lifted from his neck and her free hand guided his face towards hers. She brought her lips to his and kissed them lightly, running the tip of her tongue along the inner surfaces. Her hand moved to the back of his head and pulled his face forwards until their lips were married firmly together. Her tongue entered his mouth and danced along his, triggering a impassioned response.

Irving's ideals were smashed into little pieces as his lust began to overwhelm him. The girl gently pushed him to his back on the bed and, releasing his cock, spread open the top of his robe until his chest was fully exposed. She placed her compact, body on top of his and rubbed her stiff nipples along his chest while interposing a leg between his thighs. Her hands untied the belt to the robe and she pulled it completely open. The heat of her body atop his enflamed him and he circled her body with his arms and pulled her into him, kissing her hard. "Just this once," he told himself. "Just this one time. How can I resist it?"

Irving let the slave girl dictate to him the tempo of their lovemaking. She freed her lips from his and began to slide her body down his, dragging her fevered lips across his chest, stroking his sides. Irving knew what was coming. He was no virgin. He had had girlfriends. And he had had his cock sucked before. But he had never felt such thrilling anticipation of the event as now.

Marika washed Irving's firm belly with her lips and tongue as she slowly slid her body lower and lower. She was crouching between his thighs now and her hands circled his cock and balls caressing them lightly as her tongue played across his skin. Irving groaned with growing need to feel her mouth on his rigid rod. The girl tantalized him by running her tongue over the bulbous head and around underneath it. She teased the tiny hole at its top while running her experienced fingers along the shaft lightly. Irving raised his hand languidly and caressed her black, shiny, soft hair. When the mouth finally condescended to encompassing him, he moaned loudly as the heat and softness transferred to his manhood.

The girl slowly let her lips descend Irving's steely pole until she had absorbed it to its length. Her soft hands caressed his inner thighs. The feeling was mesmerizing and electric. Irving's body stiffened as he delighted in the exquisitely pleasurable sensations. And then the lips began to slowly ascend his stiff meat, the tongue swirling along it, and Irving groaned again.

The slave girl kept Irving in delicious agony for a long time. He had never had a blow job like this before. His mind screamed at the exquisite sensations. She seemed to know exactly when to stop her languorous attentions to his sex until his imminent crescendo receded and when to start again. Finally, it seemed like forever to the moaning, writhing technician, she brought him over the top.

Irving's body convulsed as his throbbing, jerking cock exploded. Each ejaculatory pulse sent another almost intolerable message of pleasure through his body. He felt like he was pouring out of the end of his cock into the energetic and skillful mouth that encircled him. "Ahhhhhhrgh!" he yelled, "Ahhhhhhhrgh! Ahhhhhhrgh!" as his hands seized the girl's soft, black hair. His cock seemed to go on and on, like it would never stop.

Ultimately, Irving exhausted his forces. The girl suckled his softening manhood gently, drawing out every last drop of his come. When she knew that he was done and the last echoes of his orgasm had faded, she released him and slid her body up over his until her breasts lay soothingly across his chest, her head nestled in his shoulder.

The sated man lay there a long time. His whole body was suffused with the afterglow of his climax. The girl's body was warm and comforting as she lay atop him. He had faded dreamily into near sleep when he felt her lips gently pressing against his skin. She had shifted to his side and she glided her hand across his belly and delicately surrounded his softened meat.

Patiently, soothingly, the girl's hand urged his detumesced tool close to hardness again. Irving was no stud, but he was young and in fine physical shape. Although his body was tired, his mind relished the thought of another bout with the sensual, seductive slave girl. She rose herself to her knees and Irving watched her as she ran her hand between her own thighs. Her breasts were hardened with her own lust and her face was eager and flush. She brought her hand out from between her thighs and placed her fingers beneath Irving's nose. He breathed in the unmistakable, pungent scent of her arousal.

It was all that he needed. His cock began to stiffen in the girl's nimble hand. She took him by the arm and as she lay down on the bed on her back, her thighs spread, her knees raised, her loins pushed up enticingly, she urged him to rise. Irving shucked off the robe that he had been wearing and positioned himself between the girl's inviting thighs. She was smiling, her dark eyes flashing her anticipation of pleasure. Her youthful breasts peered up at him expectantly as she took his cock and brought it to the entrance to her hairless, moistened crevasse. Irving moaned as his cock slid home and the tight, soft, hot walls of her cunt swallowed him. He lowered his body onto hers and finding her open, welcoming lips with his, began to fuck her feverishly. When he came, the girl did too, uttering a long, anguished moan, her body writhing and shuddering beneath him.

Two weeks later, Irving had long forgotten his vow not to take advantage of the availability of the many eager, subservient female bodies. The morning after he had succumbed to Marika's charms, he had fucked her again, this time with her on top. Her pussy muscles caressed his cock lovingly as she rode him. Irving was no expert, but he was sure that she took the opportunity to come twice, her head thrown back and her moans of pleasure echoing through the luxuriously appointed room. He knew that hookers often faked it, or so he had heard. But the girl's passionate responses, down to the convulsions of her sex around his stiff cock, seemed genuine indeed.

When he came back from his morning run, he had resolved to send Marika back to wherever she had come from. He had let her have her way with him and she should suffer no more punishments for failure to please him. As he had the night before, he entered his bedroom with his purpose fixed firmly in his mind.

To his surprise Marika was gone. In her place was the blond girl that he had seen in the American executive's office the day before. She was kneeling on the remade bed, her hands locked behind her. She was gagged and a chain led from her collar to a hook in the headboard. She looked up at him pleadingly. He had intended merely to release her from her bonds, but when he sat next to her on the bed, she proffered her soft, enticing breasts to him and spread her graceful thighs. He couldn't resist cupping and caressing the small, but firm mounds and then running his hand down her taut belly to her smooth, hairless sex. His fingers pried apart the delicate lips and he found her moist. He didn't bother to unbind her, but instead, casting off his running shorts and t-shirt, pushed her back down on the soft, luxurious mattress and plunged himself inside her.

Now, two weeks later, he had become inured to the abject status of the pretty, available female flesh. Every morning, after his run, a new slave girl would be mounted on his bed, bound and expectant of servicing. Twice Marika had been returned to him and he had seen her performing in the mansion lounge on a few occasions, dancing sulkily on the center stage or bent over on her knees proffering her delectable behind to one of the patrons. This morning, on his way out to the track to do the videotaping, he had seen one of the Russians leading her by a leash with her arms bound behind her and a shield gag over her mouth, down to the barracks. She was wearing a fresh decoration of angry red stripes about her body and he assumed that she had failed to please someone. It was none of his business.

His use of the girls had become more frequent and callous as time went on. He hadn't whipped any of them, but he had watched while a red headed girl with large, round breasts had been beaten for the enjoyment of the crowd one evening in the lounge. She had cried and screamed for relief from her ordeal and afterwards, his lusts boiling, Irving took one of the slave waitresses back into an alcove and ploughed her mouth. It had taken him a few days to get up the nerve to fuck one of the girls, a pleasantly full bodied British girl named Crystal, in the ass. It was something that he had never done before. The girl didn't seem to mind and moaned and cried out with delight as he dragged his cock across the tender skin of the smaller entrance. Although he had enjoyed it too, he still preferred possessing their fevered cunts and mouths instead.

There was a tall, sturdy German girl awaiting him in his room and he decided that he would wile away the time before Maureen arrived with her and the subservient brown haired girl who followed behind him.

* * * * * * * * * * * * * * *

Jake watched his tech guy walk determinedly back to the mansion. He had seen the change in the principled scientist. He had to say that he regretted it. He had also succumbed easily to the availability of so much female flesh. He knew deep down inside that he was blackening his soul, but it just seemed so normal here. And it would have been hard to maintain the respect of the native men if he had seemed reluctant to partake of the national pastime. He knew that Irving was going back to the mansion to get laid and he decided that he too would seek relief from his lusts.

Jake lived, together with his men, in the opulent carriage house that sat a few hundred yards away from the mansion. He had a bedroom on the upper floor and he knew that his slave girl, Dana was awaiting him there. She had been a gift to him from one of the Kalikastani business men who hoped to curry favor from Jake's boss. She was an American and he often wondered whether she had been brought to this god forsaken country through the slave operation in Elizabeth.

It was still going strong some seven months after he had engineered its take over. It was essential to his and Burnham's cover as ruthless Americans. It was being run by the beautiful, blonde Mary Ellen, a tough, amoral gangster in her own right. She and her crew of pretty lesbians transported the hapless, kidnapped women from all over the Eastern US to Elizabeth where they were stored and prepped for shipment via air freight to Kalikastan. Jake knew that probably 150 or so young females had found their way here since the takeover and he oftentimes wondered whether he would ever recover his moral equilibrium.

He rationalized the takeover of the operation by the fact that the girls who were being transported into slavery probably would have found their fate regardless of his actions. If he had not taken over the slaving operation, they would have been kidnapped anyway and sent on their way. But he had never thought that the operation would have gone on so long. He had expected that once they had found Maddy they would leave the country with her and shut the Elizabeth operation down. But Burnham's refusal to authorize a snatch and run with regard to Maddy had made that impossible.

Jake had never bailed on a job in his life. Once he took on a commission, he finished it, regardless of the consequences. It was a matter of pride and it had required him, at times, to do some very bad things. But that was just the way life was. However, none of the things that he had done had the moral equivalency of being responsible for the enslavement of 150 or so innocent young women, more than twenty a month. It would end soon, he hoped. But he doubted that he would ever feel clean again.

Jake walked into the carriage house through the kitchen entrance. As usual, two of his men were parked there. Curly and Martinez were sitting at the kitchen table drinking mugfuls of the local, pungent and hardy local ale and playing with two pretty slave girls. His men were getting soft. They didn't have much to do except sit around and wait for something to happen. He didn't want to send them away since he might need their muscle at some point. But whether they would be of any use when the time came was another question.

"Hey, Jake," Martinez called to him when he entered the door. Martinez was a lanky, wise cracking Hispanic, good with a knife and sharp as a tack. He had on his lap a dark skinned girl with long, black hair. Her hands were bound behind her and he was feeding her little pieces of chocolate from a candy box. She was smiling and chewing happily on a piece of caramel. Curly, a mostly reliable, lunky kind of a guy was drinking the dark, hearty ale from a tall glass. Another slave girl, one with shoulder length, sandy hair, was keeling at his feet expectantly. Her hands were resting on her thighs and her back was arched, showing off her pretty, naked breasts. Jake didn't know her name, Curly called her, naturally, Sandy, and she had been an almost constant companion for him over the last few weeks.

"Hi, boss," Curly said as he lowered his glass to the table. Jake wished that he could think of something for the boys to do, but they really weren't equipped to do much except sit around until the action started. Tucker, a large, hard as brick kind of a guy, had become enamored of two of Burnham's work ponygirls named Dora and Flora. At least he had something to do, grooming them and taking them for rides around the estate, performing little chores with their cart. Burnham liked to take them out for a spin in the afternoons sometimes and, afterwards, Tucker would rub them down and fuck them. Jake wondered, when the shit hit the fan, where Tucker's loyalties would lie. He was taciturn and had never given any doubt as to his allegiance. But when he found out that he had to leave the two, tall, big boned, pale skinned, muscular ponies behind, who knew what he would do?

Jake just gave his men a nod and passed through the kitchen to the stairs that led to the second level. He trudged up the stairs and walked to his room. When he entered the room, he saw his black haired slave girl kneeling in her cage nestled against the wall opposite his bed. She was bound and gagged and looked out at him dolefully.

Jake had had no interest in acquiring any female flesh for his own sake. It had just happened. The first one that he had owned, a pretty, big breasted, Dutch girl named Klara, had been gifted to him by an estate owner during the time that Jake was on the hunt for Maddy. He was posing as a ponygirl buyer for Burnham's estate and the owner of the estate they were visiting, in a moment of gregariousness, had gifted him the pretty, blond haired girl. At first, Jake had not known what to do with her, beyond the obvious that is. But he had become attached to the simple, sensitive young woman. She, in turn, had seemed to become attached to him. Jake was a stranger to love and he wasn't sure that was what he felt for her. He knew that as much as she appeared to be in love with him, the fact that she was his property, with the power of life and death over her, it could not really be called love. Love was what two free, independent and self actuated people had for each other, not a slave for her master.

But her care and concern and need for him had seemed real enough. It had posed him quite a dilemma. He knew that his time in Kalikastan was limited. Some day, unless he died in the attempt to rescue Maddy, he would return to the real world. What would he do with Klara then? How could he leave her behind to suffer the dismal fate of a lifetime of sexual slavery? Who knew what kind of master she would eventually fall into the hands of?

He had winced when he thought of her possible fate. But he couldn't take her with him. They would be taking a huge risk in trying to get Jackie and Maddy out as it was. If the National Commission found out, they would hunt them down like dogs. Adding Klara to the list of females to be sneaked out of the country would make everything just that much riskier. He had his men to think of too. If he took out Klara, they would undoubtedly want to rescue their favorite slave girls as well, like Curly and Sandy, or Martinez and whatever dark skinned Hispanic beauty he happened to be enamored of at the time, not to mention Tucker.

But Jake's dilemma was solved by an unhappy turn of events. Klara had been stolen. He had originally thought of her as being kidnapped, but that wasn't really the right term. People were kidnapped. Klara wasn't really a person under local law and tradition. She was property, and property was stolen, not kidnapped.

There had been no way to prove it, but Jake's hunch was that she had been stolen by Anton Drabik, Axmail Grobgy's right hand man. Jake had met Drabik for a few moments at a party at Grobgy's estate after the spring season. He had spotted Drabik right away for what he was, a stone cold killer. Sparks had flied when they met. It was Jake's theory that Klara had been kidnapped to try and get information on the real intentions of he and Burnham and their interest in Maddy, known to Drabik and Grobgy as Lightning. He imagined that Klara had suffered severe torture and interrogation at their hands. But the poor girl didn't know anything. The real purpose of their mission was a closely guarded secret. Jake had sworn that before he left Kalikastan he would kill Drabik for what he had done.

He had been gifted the pale skinned, young Dana at the same time that he had lost Klara. Jake had determined that he wouldn't make the mistake of falling for another slave girl and Dana had suffered intently because of that. While he had only beat Klara once, something that he had been ashamed of later and pledged never to do again, he had taken out his anger and frustration at losing the pleasant, loving Dutch slave girl on Dana, especially in the first days that he had possessed her.

By now his anger had muted and he had realized that his brutality to the young, enslaved American girl was brutalizing himself and so he had, for the most part, stopped. That didn't mean that her overall treatment had gotten any better. Jake refused to acknowledge her humanity, her feelings. He used her like he would any other slave girl, maybe more so. He kept her caged in his room most of the time, bound and gagged. She was released only when he used her and once a day to go to the mansion to partake in the daily exercises and reinforcements of training that all the slave girls were subject to. Slave girls were charged with keeping themselves shapely and pretty despite their callous use and he didn't want Dana to lose her voluptuous shape or alluring facial features. Besides, he knew that she needed something to look forwards to besides being cooped up all day in her little prison. He hadn't decided what he would do with her ultimately, but she was his property and he didn't want her to lose her value.

The dark haired slave girl looked out morosely at her master from behind the bright, shiny, steel bars of her cage. Dana was a college student from Ohio and had been enslaved for a little over five months. Her first master had been a caterer who supplied pretty little slave girls as party favors for the enjoyment of the guests. It had not been so bad, but being the prisoner of the callous American, had been hell. Once she had realized that she had been sold to a fellow countryman, Dana had hoped that he would sympathize with her and maybe even rescue her. But he had turned out to be mean and cruel.

She served him as best as she could and lately he had softened his abuse of her. But to keep her confined for most of the time in the little steel cage, to not let her at least have the company of her fellow slaves for comfort and commiseration was hard. Sometimes the other slave girls would sneak upstairs and talk to her. They would feed her and let her out of her cage to use the bathroom and just to stretch her aching muscles. But they did so at their own peril. And since she was kept gagged most of the time, she almost never got to talk back to them.

It was a lonely life in which hours upon hours of boredom mixed with intense periods of terror and abuse. For she never knew when her master would resume his beatings and whippings. He possessed her with a coldness that terrified her. She had tried to soften his treatment of her by using all of the considerable sexual skills that she had been taught at the point of a whip during her initial training. But no matter what she did, he remained the same. Her only hope was that someday he would leave or sell her to somebody else. She could not conceive of any situation that could be worse than belonging to him.

Jake passed the cage without acknowledging the bound woman. He kept a bottle of gin on his nightstand and he poured himself a glass without ice. He drank the fiery potion straight down. He was drinking more now than he ever had. It seemed to soothe his disobedient conscience.

And it made it easier to satisfy his lust on the bodies of the willing, but at heart, unhappy slave girls.

Jake turned to look at his property. His lust was up from watching Chocolate and he pulled off his t-shirt, boots and pants without ceremony. He stepped over to the cage and released the lock, ordering the girl out with a motion of his head.

Dana dipped her head and crawled free of her prison. While she was happy to be out, she was not happy that it was for the purposes of serving her owner's lust. Who knew what he would do to her today? He still beat her from time to time, not for anything she did wrong, that she could tell, but more for his enjoyment or to assuage some inner demon that possessed him. She could never tell whether he was primed to cause her pain or pleasure. What would it be today?

Dana rose to her feet slowly. Her cramped leg and back muscles ached as she stretched them. She stood about six or so inches shorter than the man and she looked up at him now fearfully. She tried to push her heavy, round breasts out at him invitingly and she softened her gaze to attempt to convey her willingness to serve him. But he just looked back at her coldly and ordered her to get on the bed.

Jake took another shot of gin before he climbed up onto the mattress. It burned going down and felt good. He reached behind the girl and loosened her bound arms only to reconnect them to the ring on the back of her collar. Her new pose made her breasts rise as if in greeting to him. He ran his hands over them, appreciating their exquisite combination of softness and firmness. He tweaked the fat nipples at their ends until they stood up. He wanted his slave girl good and aroused when he fucked her. He wanted to hear her come and watch her writhe and squirm as her orgasm overtook her. He placed his lips on one of her teats and sucked at it softly, running his tongue around the bumpy areola while his hand massaged the other breast. The girl, who had been tense and rigid when he had seized her body, began to ease her posture and give herself into her pleasure.

Slave girls were taught very early their duty to respond to their masters' ministrations. A slave girl who was not passionate was worthless. It was not enough to energetically service the bodies of her the men who took possession of her. She must respond passionately to their embraces, make her pussy lush with anticipation, surrender herself over to lust. Dana had been beaten repeatedly until she learned how to unleash her desires. She took her mind to a place where there were no slave girls, no masters. Back to a small motel room in Ohio where she and her boyfriend used to spend the night in passionate embraces. She brought the feelings of happiness and lust to her mind and pretended that it was now, that it was his mouth that suckled her sensitive teat, that it was his hand that was caressing her breast, his body's heat that she felt next to her.

Jake's cock was hard with anticipation of his use of his slave girl's body. He shifted his mouth to her other breast and slid his hand down her taut belly to the crux of her thighs. She was kneeling up and she spread her legs obediently to give him access. He rubbed the twin, hairless lips gently, absorbing the soft sensations of his fingers exploring her sex. He ran his hand over the insides of her thighs, letting his fingers dance upon her tender flesh.

The girl sighed as her juices began to rise. She had closed her eyes and focused on the pleasurable sensations that the man's hands and mouth were bringing her. When his hand took possession of her smooth, hairless slit, she pressed it against him and sighed again in anticipation of his exploration of the moist cleft in between.

Jake was encouraged by the girl's sounds of developing passion. But he wanted more. He took her by the shoulders and pushed her onto her back on the mattress. He spread her legs widely and placed his body between them. His hungry eyes took in her beauteous form. Her breasts shimmered, full and ripe. Her belly was flat and tight and bore the tattoo of her training house, a snarling brown fox with bared, fierce teeth and a long, bushy tail. Her name, in blue Cyrillic letters adorned her chest. Her torso was graceful and smooth. She looked up at him apprehensively. Her blue eyes sparkled in a sea of white.

Jake took the girl's breasts in his hands and squeezed them gently. He took her nipples between his fingers and thumbs and pinched them until the girl moaned with the beginnings of pain. Yes, he could bring her pleasure or pain, whatever he wanted. He let the girl hang on the precipice, wondering which he would bring her today. It would be a simple matter to go to the wall and remove one of the cruel implements of torture that hung there. He could make her lie there obediently, her legs spread and raised while he pummeled her defenseless cunt and thighs. Or he could pierce her with his steel hard sword of flesh, bringing her wave after wave of pleasure.

The girl's chest rose and fell as she anxiously awaited her fate. Her head rested on her bound hands affixed behind her neck. Her eyes were widened with fear. But today was not a day for pain. It was a day for pleasure. Jake lowered his lips to the girl's breasts and suckled one teat and then the other. He began to lower his body to the foot of the bed, kissing her belly, running his tongue over her fierce tattoo and then over the delicate, pale skin above her loins. He wanted to hear her moan and groan with pleasure before he fucked her. She was like an instrument that he could play, her vocalization of her lust music to his ears.

Lifting the girl's graceful thighs with his hands, Jake let his tongue drift along the outside of her flush gash. He lapped the skin between her thighs and the folds of her sex and then over the engorged lips themselves. He was drunk with the smell of her arousal. Her moisture glistened between her nether lips. He could see the glimmering medallions affixed to their base which recorded her as his property, on one, the symbol of his ownership, a broadwinged eagle, its talons lifted to snatch its prey, on the other, her name and his on opposite sides. Klara had worn similar medals. But she had worn them proudly. For a moment, a wave of remorse spread through the impassioned fixer. She was probably buried in some shallow grave somewhere in the Kalikastani forest not far from the Grobgy estate, her body inconvenient evidence of Drabik's crime against him. Jake shook off his momentary relapse into sorrow. That was all past now. She was gone and that was that. He needed his lust and the lust of this girl to help him forget her.

Jake drew his tongue along the length of the moaning woman's cleft and teased the tender bud at its tip. The girl's pudenda rose to meet him as the sensations of pleasure shot through her. He took the sensitive nubbin between his teeth and lips and alternated between a gentle, prolonged suckle and a sharp, intense bite. The girl gasped through her gag as she endured his attentions. Her hips were shifting in an increasingly agitated rhythm.

He delved his tongue deeply into her gushing canal and found the sensitive spot on its roof, teasing and stroking it until the girl's moans became hard and strained. He gripped her thighs tightly with his hands and took possession of her hardened clit once again with his lips, flicking the little button with his tongue again and again. Her body was in desperate motion now and her moans were deep and loud. Suddenly, her body began to convulse and shake as her orgasm over took her. "Mmmmmmmmm! Mmmmmmmmmmmmm! Mmmmmmmmmmmmm!" she groaned into her gag. Her legs quivered and her back arched as the pleasure of her climax seized her body and mind. Her moans became staccato, echoing each intense convulsion of her cunt, "Mmmm! Mmmm! Mmmm! Mmmm! Mmmmm!"

When her body's writhing began to slow, Jake let up his ministrations, letting the girl ease back from her frantic contortions. But he did not stop. He let his tongue and lips flow over the outside of her blood filled, hairless labia and over the insides of her thighs until he felt her body relax. And then he started again.

He made the impassioned slave girl come three times, each time waiting until her convulsions had subsided to begin again. Driven to almost painful ecstasy, she tried to close her thighs to deny him access to the source of her exquisite torture, but his hands kept them firmly apart.

Finally, when the slave girl was on the receding crest of her third climax, he could hold his own lust back no more. He raised himself above the panting, sweat covered girl and slid his hard, thick cock between her fevered lower lips. Her pussy was hot and flush with her arousal. She groaned as he possessed her, her eyes looking up at him desperately, her hands struggling for freedom behind her head. Jake rasped his cock across her clit and the girl began to thrust her hips back at him with all the intensity that she could muster. He plunged to her depths and then withdrew again and again, pounding his hips against hers. His eyes burned into hers fiercely. "I own you!" they said. "I possess your flesh! I can do anything I want with you!"

Seeing the harsh, impassioned gaze of her master, the girl trembled with fear and pleasure. His cock sawed at her loins piston like, drawing her nearer and nearer to another body wrenching orgasm. Fucking with her boyfriend had never been like this. It was the sole consolation of her miserable life. None of the masters had ever fucked her like this cruel, unfathomable man. Why didn't he just let her serve him like all the other slave girls? She would bring him pleasure in exchange. But she knew that only the intense combination of fear and lust could bring her this high. Only his impersonal, ruthless use of her could drive her to the peaks of pleasure that he brought her.

If she had to be a chattel, open to those who owned her flesh, wasn't it better to have this compensation? Wasn't it better than the cold, indifferent fucks she had received when working as a whore for her prior owner? Alone and bored in her tiny steel prison for hour after hour it did not seem so. But now, as her pussy prepared to bring her another round of intense, mind numbing contractions of pleasure, she would say yes again and again.

Jake's cock exploded inside the girl's womb. He groaned and his body shook with his convulsions. The girl's legs wrapped around his back as she came too. Her pussy's contractions squeezed his cock feverishly. He seized the girl's long, black hair with his hands and glared into her widespread eyes as he poured his essence into her. He saw there the girl's surrender to him, her acknowledgment of his mastery of her physical self. Finally, his cock's pulses began to wane and he lay his head down over her shoulder and let his body relax.

The lovers, if you could call them that, lay entwined, exhausted, as the light faded from outside through the windows of the room, each of them lost in their own universe of thought. Their bodies glowed with the aftereffects of their sexual exertions. When Jake finally stirred himself from his reverie, he sat up on the bed and poured himself another long shot of gin.

While well enamored of other kinds of firewater, gin was Jake's special favorite. Whenever he drank it he thought of Kipley's reference to, "mad dogs and Englishmen". To him it was like handling a loaded gun. He never knew where it would take him. Some of his fiercest drunks had been on gin. But that had been mostly in the early days. He had too much mileage on him and had made too many enemies to allow himself more than the occasional bender. He felt like going on one now. But he wouldn't. Not here. He had promised himself a 'lulu' when this job was done. For now, though, he needed some other way of releasing his tensions.

Tossing the clear, mean liquid back, Jake put down his glass and looked at the shiny, perspiration covered body of his slave girl. She was still mired in the aftereffects of her series of orgasms. He would need to wake her up.

Jake got up and took from the wall a foot long length of chain with clips on both ends. He returned to the bed and sat down next to the now aware female. She was looking at him with the look she got when she sensed that things were going to turn unpleasant. Her body trembled as Jake ran his hand down her thigh, over her knee and down her shin to her ankle. She wore the regulation slave bracelet on it. It had a convenient ring embedded in the leather and Jake fastened one end of the chain to it. Taking both of the girl's ankles in hand, he raised them until her legs were bent back and her feet were at the level of her upper chest. He drew the chain through a ring in the front of the girl's collar and connected its free end to her other ankle. Her legs were raised and spread open wide, revealing her still enflamed cleft and the little brown star between her rear cheeks. Her posture also made available the tender inside of her pale, firm thighs.

The girl had given out a low whine from behind her gagged lips when Jake had begun the process of imprisoning her legs. She knew what was to come. Sweat broke out on her brow and her pretty blue eyes reflected her dismay. Jake caressed the soft skin of her inner thighs with his hard, strong hand while drinking in the girl's terror. His cock had begun to stir already.

Jake stepped up from the bed and selected an 18" long tasseled, leather whip from the wall. Its thin strands were hard, having been cured in vinegar and water. It would bring the girl pain, but, if handled delicately, would not mar her. After an hour or so, there would only be the memory of her torment remaining as a reminder of her abuse. Jake didn't like to see the evidence of his evil on the girl; it tended to grate on his conscience when he saw her in the mornings. He couldn't help his dark moods and he often regretted his cruelty to the girl when he had taken his abuse of her too far. But this whip had proven just the right tool to use to drive her to the extremes of pain while camouflaging the evidence of his growing depravity.

Jake positioned himself at the end of the bed where he could get a clear shot at the girl's exposed intimacies. Her hairless pudenda and soft rear cheeks were proffered to him invitingly. The girl had begun to sob softly. She knew better than to protest or try to beg. It would only make things worse. She would have to endure it like any other slave girl, saving her voice for her screams and moans of pain.

The first blow of the whip landed on the inside of the girl's right thigh. It made a loud 'crack' as it struck her flesh and the girl's body jumped at contact. She gave out a loud moan of pain, loud enough to emerge from her gag and fill the room. The second blow landed across her left thigh. Her body shuddered and her legs flinched as she absorbed it, matching her movements with a piteous sound from her gagged mouth. The third landed across her defenseless, plump labial lips and the girl gave out a screech, her legs pulling helplessly against their confinements.

Again and again Jake pummeled the girl's delightful flesh. His lust grew with each slap of the cruel instrument on her flesh. After about five or six strokes, her skin began to turn a glowing red, proof of the efficacy of his efforts. Her screams were loudest when he laid the hard strands of leather over her puffy, engorged slit and when he purposely placed his aim at the dainty, puckered rear hole.

The girl's thighs and rear were a fiery red when Jake put the whip aside. He was sweating heavily from his endeavors and from his growing passion. The girl had squirmed and cried on the bed, but had made no effort to escape or evade her unwarranted punishment. There were crueler, fiercer instruments of pain on the walls and she knew that such behavior would result in the exchange of the relatively mild weapon that Jake had been wielding with one of them.

Jake's cock was hard and engorged with his fevered blood when he climbed up on the bed. He rose above the girl's abject form and targeted his manhood at the girl's battered and sore rear entrance. She was still crying from her ordeal, but was aware enough of her duties to soften the muscles there in anticipation of her master's penetration. Her entrance was still tight and Jake had to force his way across the small, sensitive ring until it expanded enough to let him thrust his prick deep into the girl's bowels.

The pressure of the tight flesh around the shaft of his cock was exhilarating and the hot, soft, murky depths of her innards enflaming. Jake's mind clouded with pleasure as he rasped his cock back and forth along the small opening. He looked down and saw the girl's frantic eyes peering back, her elbows splayed to the sides of her head, her lower face obscured by the sound deadening gag which covered her lips and chin. Jake placed his hand on the girl's reddened slit and began to massage the tiny bud at its top, delving his thumb inside her crevasse and spreading her moisture over it. He fucked her with long, slow strokes while he excited her.

The slave girl's breasts shifted up and down deliciously each time he thrust his hips against the girl's angry red rear globes. Her eyes had softened now as her arousal was advancing. She was a well trained slut, he had to give her that. She was delivering to her master what was his, her passion and lust. In spite of her damaged, burning flesh, she was succumbing to the teasing of her sex and her moans of pain had turned to cries of pleasure.

He had grown to know her body well in the weeks that he had owned her and he was timing himself carefully to deliver his hot seed into her bowels until she succumbed to her needs. Suddenly, he saw her eyes widen and roll back. Her body began to shudder and her large, firm, pale breasts shook, their tips hard and dark red. Jake groaned loudly as he felt his cock begin to pulse and throb deep within the girl. He quickened his thrusts as his pleasure shot through him like a lightning bolt. He spurted his essence inside the moaning slave and his body tensed almost beyond endurance.

When his ejaculations slowed and finally faded, Jake's body collapsed on top of the moaning, still shuddering girl.

CHAPTER FOUR
THE DODO BIRD

Burnham watched Jake and Irving march off in opposite directions. They were both pains in the ass in their individual ways, but both necessary for the completion of his plans. He would tolerate them as long as he had to. There would be a clean sweep at the end of the fall pony racing season, you could be sure of that.

He had spent his life pulling silver linings out of dark, grey clouds and Maddy's kidnapping had proved to be no exception. Of course he was concerned for the fate of his niece. But there were larger concerns. If she had listened to him, she wouldn't have been kidnapped in the first place. He wanted her to attend an Ivy League school, at his expense of course. But no, she wanted to be independent. Well, she had paid the price all right. For seven months or so, she had been suffering the life of an abject beast, whipped and abused on a daily basis. It was taking much longer than he had thought it would to rescue her, it was regrettable. But there was the bigger picture to consider. She had already suffered through the worst of it anyway, being dehumanized. She could certainly hang in a little bit longer.

Burnham had started out with nothing and had built his empire with his two fists: resolute determination and ruthlessness towards his opponents. Corners had to be cut here and there, people eased out of the way, or, if not exactly eased, removed as problems one way or the other. Jake had helped him out before and done his work efficiently and without moral qualm. He sensed, however, that the 'fixer' had just about reached his limits of ethical compromise. Well, he could last a little longer too. He liked Jake, he really did, but if he thought that he would interfere with his plans, he was sadly mistaken.

The billionaire watched Giorgi guide Chocolate over to the ponybarn where she was disconnected from her new cart. She would be led over to the ponygirl camp near the race track for the night and be brought back tomorrow for more work. He was damned if he was ever going to give up one of the best racing ponies in the country. Jake's concern over his promise to the former African American woman was quaint in light of all the other women that his efforts had caused to be brought here for enslavement.

The female was probably better off as a ponygirl anyway than as a hooker, high class or otherwise. She was healthy, in great physical shape. As a hooker, she had been exposed to the possibility of untimely and sudden death from a crazed john or some nasty drug dealer. As far as he was concerned, the girl had sold her soul long before she ever agreed to come to Kalikastan. Anyway, the decision to keep her had been made and that was that. If Jake didn't like it, he would just have to be dealt with.

Right now, Burnham had bigger fish to fry. Peter Wong, the Eurasian gangster was due today with a shipment of goods. It was to be the first of many. It was part of Burnham's new International syndicate. He had established, with the blessing of the National Commission of course, a kind of golden triangle between American underworld figures, renegade Chinese governmental officials and the Southeast Asian cartels represented by

Wong. Burnham would be the banker for the concern, investing the mounds of cash to be generated in legitimate markets all around the world.

It was nice to be in a country which knew how to treat business. Even the American government had agreed to look the other way. The agreement to house a CIA interrogation center in the country as well as the ability to allow American companies to hide their bribes to foreign officials from federal banking regulators was the quid pro quo for accepting the 'drafting' in the national interest, of course, a small number of young, American females on a regular basis to round out the bargain. Their service to their country was a small price to play for the restoration of American products to competitiveness. Imagine trying to outlaw the only thing that could assure American companies fair treatment in global markets. It was like running a race with one leg lopped off. No empire had ever been preserved without sacrifice.

Burnham had already established several accounts for major American corporations, accounts which American regulators would never get the chance to audit. There was a teleconference scheduled with New York in a few minutes and Burnham needed to hurry back to the mansion to avoid being late for it. He had enjoyed the show with Chocolate but it was time to get back to business.

The tall, heavyset American walked briskly back to the mansion. He walked up the chiseled granite steps and entered the building through the large, oaken wooden doors. A pair of Russians wearing their signature black t-shirts with the image of Burnham's estate emblem on the left side of their chests, the angry, red fanged mastiff's head, had nodded at him as he climbed the steps. They were equipped with M-16's. Burnham knew that the Ruski's preferred their own standard automatic rifle, the Kalashnikov, to the M-16, but it was a matter of national pride for Burnham to have them carrying the American weapon. Although the Russian automatic rifle was believed generally to be more reliable and simpler to care for, he wanted the heavier caliber and firepower of the M-16. If the shit ever hit the fan with another of the outlaw gangs in the country, he wanted his guys to be able to blast them off the face of the earth.

The doors to the Burnham mansion led into a vast entrance hallway with white marble floors and tall colonnades. Pretty, little, naked slave girls stood at the base of each one, an enticing, erotic display of Burnham's wealth and power. In the middle of the Grand Hall, as it was referred to, two women wrestled in passionate embrace on a large, circular, padded platform. They were changed every hour or so. A guard stood in the hallway armed with a whip in the event that their lusts flagged.

Giving the writhing sluts a disinterested glance, Burnham made his way up the broad, marble steps to the second floor where his private office was. Outside of it, sitting at a desk, was his former secretary, Libby, who he had rechristened 'Betty'. She had known too much about his activities to be left behind in New York. And when he found out that she had secreted away details of his more outré financial transactions for purposes of blackmail, he had determined that she would pay a special price for her betrayal.

Betty had been an attractive, full chested, fortyish chestnut haired woman. He had had many a comment from visitors to his executive suite about her comeliness. He had often wondered what it would be like to fuck her and to play with her delightful, prominent orbs, but in the delicate legal atmosphere which governed employer-employee sexual relations back in the States, he had denied himself the opportunity to find out. Here, of course, things were different.

The shapely secretary had always dressed stylishly, if conservatively. Her hair was lush and full, down to her shoulders and her face had clean, handsome details. She was a model of efficiency and a damn good administrative assistant. Her duties now were somewhat more limited although rather more demanding. He had enticed her here under false pretenses and than had proceeded to enslave her. But he had done more than that.

Her head had been shaved and he had had her upper body covered with tattoos. They were specifically designed to suggest multicolored feathers, all over her belly and breasts, her back, her arms and even her head and face. She wore a thick golden ring through her nose. Her hands were kept chained through a ring in the front of her brass collar, forcing her hands up and her elbows out to her sides. When she stood in front of you, it gave the effect of her having little wings, like a huge dodo bird. He had left her lower body unmarked and had left her wiry, brown, pubic bush in place. Her hairiness below accentuated her nudity and her pale, shapely, unmarked legs contrasted sharply with her multicolored, feathery looking upper body.

It had been Burnham's intention to humiliate her and he had been successful in this endeavor. The guards loved to play with her when she wasn't manning her post in front of his office and he always brought her out for special occasions, making her circulate among his guests holding a little tray containing hor d'ouvres. She was the subject of much amusement and always ended the evening well used.

As Burnham rose up the stairs he could see her spread legs and her furry loins underneath her frontless desk. She was under instructions to keep her well toned, pale thighs open so that her open pussy would be the first thing that anyone would see when they ascended the stairs. The sight of the available sex reminded Burnham of his raised lust from watching his brown skinned ponygirl mouth off her diminutive driver a little while ago. It had been some time since he had given the bird woman his carnal attentions and he decided to 'invite' her into his office.

The former executive secretary watched her cruel master and erstwhile employer as he approached her. Her eyes were doleful as she was always conscious of her absurd, dehumanized appearance. This was the man who had done it to her, the man who had forced her at gunpoint to beg to be his slave rather than face execution for her 'crimes'. She had never intended to use the documents that his men had found in her apartment unless necessary to save herself. Sooner or later, she had believed, the authorities would catch up with Burnham and she would be implicated in his financial chicaneries. It was to be merely a bargaining chip to avoid her own prosecution. But her efforts to protect herself had brought about her cruel enslavement instead.

"How are you today, Betty?" Burnham asked as he reached the top of the stairs and approached her desk. Betty couldn't answer since she wore a leather shield gag across her mouth. There was no telephone on her desk, just a little speaker and two buttons. Whenever a visitor arrived, Betty would lean over and press the right hand button which set off a buzzer in Burnham's office. There was a camera behind her desk and Burnham would look up at his monitor and instruct Betty over the speaker whether to let the man in or to have him wait. The other button opened the lock to Burnham's office.

"Buzz me in, slut," Burnham instructed her. He liked to watch her bend over and struggle to reach the button without dragging her delicious, large, round breasts on the desk top. It was impossible, and as she leaned over now obediently, her nipples kissed the desk's surface, compressing her colorful mounds. A chain led from the ring in her nose to a ring embedded in the desk and, after the door had been unlocked, Burnham reached down and freed it.

"Come in with me, Betty," Burnham ordered her churlishly. "I want to give you some 'dicktation'."

The pun was Burnham's idea of a joke and he chuckled as he said it. Burnham often laughed at his own jokes. And so did everyone around him. It wasn't that he wanted to be surrounded by sycophants, he just liked it when his minions reminded him of how clever he was.

The weirdly decorated woman rose from her chair and followed her chief tormentor into his office. It was a large room as befitting Burnham's importance and wealth. He had a large, leather covered, dark oak desk and a big, black leather chair behind it. There were comfortable, elegant, richly upholstered, English Regency chairs set in front and a dark walnut sideboard along the wall. The rug was a plush beige and the walls were white. Three four by four cages lined the wall behind the desk. Only one was occupied today, a frightened, pretty, blond haired girl ensconced in it. She was fresh from her training in the new facility that Burnham had built and which he would visit in a little while. Burnham had played with her this morning and she bore stark, red lines about her torso as evidence of it. Her hands were locked behind her and she was gagged.

Burnham took a seat in his chair behind the desk and motioned Betty to her knees next to him. She sank dutifully to the rug, her eyes peering up at him with a combination of fear and hate. He ran his hands over her smooth, garishly decorated, hairless head. "What's the matter Betty?" he teased her. "Don't you want to suck your master's cock? I could send you back to the training cells if you'd like. You'd get lots of cock there."

The cruel American ran his hands along her strangely decorated face and then reached down and seized her breasts. "You have great tits for a forty year old whore, Betty," he told her. "But they're just a little saggy. Maybe I'll have the doctor firm them up a little bit. Would that be okay with you? And maybe I'll think of a few more things for him to do to you like remove your teeth. I bet you'd have a lot of fun gumming cocks all the time."

The cruel billionaire tightened his grips on Betty's breasts until he was squeezing them hard. The forlorn former secretary whined from the pain and from fear that Burnham would carry out his threat. She knew that he could do whatever he wanted to her and there was not a power in the world that could stop him. She could hardly believe the nightmare that she had found herself in. Maybe it would have been better if she had let him shoot her that first day many weeks ago. She had been whipped and beaten and fucked by dozens of men. She didn't know how long she had been locked up down in the training cells. Before the new facility had been built, they were down in the basement of the mansion. She had never been in the newly constructed training center, but she was sure that it was a hell on earth. She never wanted to go back. She would obey her callous master without question.

Burnham had slid his hands down to the ends of her aching breasts and was pinching her nipples harshly. Involuntary tears formed in her eyes as she tried to resist the urge to pull away from him. She knew that he needed only the slightest provocation to beat her. She wanted to avoid his wrath at all costs. A moan escaped her gagged mouth and her eyes looked up at the man beggingly. Somehow she would escape, she promised herself. Either that or she would kill herself and this demonic abuser of women as well if she could. She knew that if she tried and failed, she would suffer a torment beyond anything that she had ever imagined. He would probably boil her in oil or roast her over a fire. So she would have to make sure that when she made her move it would succeed. For now, she would endure.

Burnham had tired of watching his slave squirm in pain. "Get under the desk," he ordered her roughly as he released her pained nipples. "I've got five minutes before the conference and if you don't get me off before then, I'll whip your flesh raw. Got it?"

Betty nodded forlornly. Burnham released the strap behind the woman's head that held her gag in place. The leather shield had attached a large, thick, penis shaped wad of leather and he extricated it from her mouth. The shield gag had covered a large, round ring of stiff leather that sat behind the woman's teeth. It held her lips open in a fixed 'O'. This way her mouth was always ready for cocksucking. She would have to use her tongue and the back of her throat to bring her master to climax.

Betty crawled under the desk and crouched in the well in the middle. Burnham had loosened his pants and pulled his hardening meat out. He spread his legs and leaned back in his chair. "Five minutes, Betty," he reminded her. "Now do your job like a good slut."

Betty took the man's thick cock in her hands and began to stoke it to firmness. When it became engorged with blood, she aimed the center of the ring gag at it and subsumed it with her mouth. She ran her tongue around its bulbous head and then pushed her head down until it pierced the entrance to her throat.

Burnham sighed as he felt the hot, moist envelope surround his rigid pole. He placed his hands on the bald, tattooed head as Betty began to plunge her head up and down feverishly on it. The man had said five minutes and she knew that he meant it.

The room echoed with the sounds of Betty's intense attentions to Burnham's cock. The hard, thick instrument made a squishing noise each time that she brought it home past the rear of her mouth. She tried to remain silent, but her throat emitted a low 'ga, ga, ga' sound every time the hard wand of flesh struck home. Her hands, chained to the ring in her collar, had just enough reach so that she could place them on the man's heavy, hard thighs.

Desperately, the frightened bird woman bobbed her head up and down. Burnham could feel his juices rising. He closed his eyes and tilted his head back, enjoying the feel of the tight ring of the woman's esophagus. He had become quite a cocksman since he had assumed the role of a slave owner. He knew that he could control his crisis much longer than the five minutes than he had given the strange looking creature that was serving him so frantically. But he had a videoconference coming up and he wanted to get nice and relaxed before it started. Watching the ponygirl had raised his lusts and he needed to take the edge off. But he would hold out as long as he could until the time for the conference.

Betty's stomach tightened as she went on and on with her oral efforts. She couldn't tell how much time had passed and it seemed that she would never get him off. She gave out a whine as she redoubled her efforts. "Please come! Please!" she thought. "Please!"

The impassioned man glanced at his watch. There were about forty five seconds to go. He let his body relax and gave in to the pleasurable sensations. His balls tightened and he felt the familiar surge in them. He moaned as he sensed his completion approaching. "Arrrrgh! Arrrrrrgh!" he yelled out as his fevered cock began to throb and spurt in the woman's mouth. He gripped her head fiercely and pressed it down on his pole, lodging his pulsing meat deep in her throat. "Arrrrrrgh! Arrrrrrgh!" he exclaimed as his pleasure shot through him. And Jake had wanted him to give this all up, he thought fleetingly. No fucking way!

Betty was crying and struggling for breath when he finally allowed her to raise her head. She took a deep, tortured breath and then coughed and sputtered.

"Keep my cock in your mouth, slut. I want to be hard again when I'm done with my conference," Burnham told her. He pressed a button on his desk and the large, flat, color monitor on the far wall came to life.

Four men sat on either side of a long conference table. They were dressed in sharply tailored business suits and their postures and demeanors oozed power and privilege. The tinges of grey hair and softness to their features bespoke men used to comfort and access to the finer pleasures of life. They were all looking up at the camera expectantly.

"Gentlemen," Burnham started, "I assume that no introductions are needed."

The man on the right closest to the camera replied. "No, they are not. My associates and I are anxious to get down to business."

"Good." Burnham answered. "You have all received the proposals and have confirmed your commitment. This meeting is for the sole purpose of giving you my personal assurances as to the security of your investments and my guarantee that I will pursue your interests diligently. The money has been received as well as your coded instructions. It will be distributed accordingly."

"How do we know that our money will reach the intended beneficiaries," one of the men asked.

"I can only give you my personal guaranty on that, Bob," Burnham relied. Bob was the chairman of a major oil and gas exploration company. His firm was interested in obtaining leases to certain offshore parcels in a small, Southeast Asian country. John and William, the first man who spoke, represented a leading aerospace corporation which was bidding for the right to sell passenger jets to a fledgling African nation. Donald ran an entertainment empire and was seeking development rights to a stretch of pristine coastline in the Caribbean for a gambling resort. All of the men needed their gratuities to reach the right people in a way that would not come back to haunt them.

"All I can say," Burnham added, "is that the proof will be in the pudding. The only visible confirmation that you will have is when your contracts are successfully awarded. I have been able to confirm in each instance that the people we are dealing with have the authority to bring about the results that you desire. I have made certain, let's call them security arrangements, so that should there be a default on the other end, retribution will be swift and sure and your investments will be returned forthwith."

"So you are underwriting the transactions, eh, Burnham? Is that what you're telling us?" It was William speaking. He had a round face untrammeled by signs of age or toil. Like all of the men, he had climbed the corporate ladder many years ago and now sat at the pinnacle of commercial power. Men like this didn't ever worry where their next meal was coming from or that the vicissitudes of economics would deprive them of wealth. Their only concern was 'more'.

"You are all paying substantial premiums for the privileges of utilizing my services. Think of it as a form of insurance," Burnham answered him.

Betty, unseen to the men on the video screen, was still holding her master's tumescent cock in her mouth. Her tongue played with it leisurely, just enough to bring a steady flow of pleasurable sensations to him. His right hand rested on her smooth, bald head.

The first man who had spoken looked at his 'associates', as he called them, and then turned back to Burnham. "I believe that we are all satisfied at the arrangements, Burnham. As I'm sure that you're aware, we have access to, as you call them, certain security arrangements, as well. If anything goes wrong we will not rely on any judicial remedies, if you understand me."

"I am certainly cognizant of your resources, William. I am certain that you will never have need of them," Burnham responded.

The men all looked at each other and nodded their acceptance. Burnham smiled. "Now that that has been concluded, I hope that you will all avail yourselves of my invitation to enjoy my hospitality here in Kalikastan. I have arranged a special flight for you next week. I have purchased a small hotel in the heart of the capital where you will be able to enjoy the benefit of our local entertainment resources. Believe me, you'll have the time of your lives."

The men on the screen all relaxed their corporate visages and smiled. They knew exactly what Burnham was talking about. In fact, all through the conference, their gazes had been shifting back and forth from their host to the cages visible behind him. The naked, little blond girl had been peering up at them forlornly. Her gagged face and her bound arms needed no explanation. The men all nodded their heads gleefully.

"I'm sure that I speak for all when I say that your invitation is most gracious and we look forward to sampling your hospitality," William replied.

"Oh, and Donald," Burnham added, "while you're here, we can speak some more about providing your new resort with our special brand of entertainment. I've already broached the subject with the local authorities and you'll have no problems on that score."

Donald licked his lips in seeming anticipation of being the owner of a bevy of fine, female flesh. "I'm intrigued by the possibilities, Burnham. See you next week."

"Good afternoon, gentlemen, or should I say good morning in the States. I look forward to seeing you in person soon," Burnham replied, a smug, satisfied smile on his face.

Burnham shut off the video monitor and sat back in his chair. The tantalizing sensations from the tongue on his cock had become almost unbearable. It had been an effort to maintain his composure while talking to the American CEO's. His tool was hard again and he was anxious for another bout with his birdwoman. He slid his chair back from the desk and the creature in the well of his desk followed it dutifully.

"Good work, Betty," Burnham told her. "You've become a real fine slut. But I want to fuck you now and so let go of my cock and get up on the desk."

Betty/Libby had been listening to the teleconference while she was addressing her oral attentions to her master's tool. She was shocked at what she had heard. Burnham had become a monster. His depredations had gone far beyond financial chicanery. Somebody had to stop him. But she knew that it wouldn't be her. She was ashamed at her own cowardice and powerlessness. Of course, with her hands almost continuously chained and confined before her, there was little that she could do. But even if she could, she was so afraid of being beaten and tortured that she doubted that she had the courage to act. She cursed herself for her abjectness in obeying the man's callous commands. Was this life she led so precious that she feared losing it? Was there any realistic hope that she would ever be saved?

At first, she had pinned her hopes on Jake. She had known him from before and, in fact, was the one who had put the call through to him when Burnham had retained him in the search for Maddy. He had been present when her former employer had enslaved her. Since then, he had used her several times, gently and appreciatively, not like the Russian men who taunted and humiliated her.

Afterwards, she had begged Jake, in desperate, whispered pleas, not to leave her behind when he left. He was noncommittal. And so even that shred of hope had gone. She would die in Kalikastan. The only question was how much terror and torment she would suffer before it happened. She had shivered with fear when Burnham had suggested that he would have her mouth denuded of teeth or alter her breasts. He knew that the man was capable of it. Her only recourse was to pray that it wouldn't happen.

Obediently, Betty rose to her feet and hopped up on the desk, ass first. Burnham had fucked her here many times and she knew the drill. She lay back on its leather covered expanse and spread her legs, placing her feet on the desk to either side of her. Her fur covered mons was exposed to the man's depredations. She rolled her eyes back into her head and tried to bring herself to a place where she could lubricate her sex as she had been taught. She knew that Burnham would be angered if he had to force his way in.

When Betty felt her owner's hand on her moss covered cleft, she began to think of loving caresses she had once experienced. There had been a boy in college who had driven her mad with lust. She tried to pretend that the hand belonged to him, a tall, broad shouldered, Italian boy. He had been a wrestler and his body was firm and well muscled. He had a dick that could last forever and he had fucked her for hours on end. They had broken up when she had discovered that he was giving the same treatment to her roommate.

As Burnham's hand began to probe her loins, Betty felt her pussy begin to moisten. She had in her mind the handsome, impassioned face of her college lover as he leaned over her, probing her fevered crevasse with his powerful dick. She had had long, flowing hair then, firm, ripe, ample breasts that stood out on their own. Her hips had been a little less wide and her belly as flat as Kansas. He was not her first, but he was close to it. Later in life, when she learned how rare a really good fuck was, she had chided herself for her simplistic morality and foolish sensitivity. So what if he fucked the whole sorority. A night with his cock had been a night spent in heaven and no man had ever measured up to him again.

Burnham gazed down at the supine form of his tattooed secretary. He gave a little chuckle as he reflected at how odd she looked. It was fun to rub his hand over her wiry, brown bush. All the other slave girls had their loins clean shaved. It made their pudenda seem invitingly available. Ironically, Betty's thick jungle of pubic hair gave her, in contrast, an obscene, animalistic look, especially in contrast to her colorful, painted upper body and her pale, clean, white thighs.

The birdwoman's slit was moist and dilated now. Burnham's cock was hard and needy as he ran his thumb inside her, spreading her moisture over her labial lips. He rubbed her stiffened nubbin of flesh at the apex of her sex, making the creature squirm and moan with lust. He took his cock in his other hand and stepped closer to the desk. He dragged the head of his hard piece along the divide between her engorged nether lips, covering it with her moisture. The sensation of her inner heat transferred to the tip of his cock sent a wave of pleasure through him. There was nothing like fucking a slave girl, flesh that you owned and owed no duty towards. If she was allowed to experience pleasure, it was only because it served his own, gave him a thrill to see her in the throes of passion. Slowly, he edged his rigid meat forwards, sinking his flesh within her. His cock pushed aside her blood filled lips and found acceptance within. As he sank further and further into the hot, soft envelope, the birdwoman groaned with lust.

Burnham began to fuck her with long, deliberate, slow strokes. He leaned over and took a stiffened nipple in his mouth, sucking on it hard and strong. His arms had circled around her pale, gracious thighs and his hands were laying on the desk, forcing Betty's legs back and up. He bit down hard on her nipple, causing the woman to moan with pain as his cock continued to torment her. He shifted to her other teat and, after teasing it with his tongue and sucking at it, gave it the same treatment as the other, sinking his teeth firmly into the woman's sensitive flesh.

"Ooooooooooo!" Betty cried out through her ring gagged mouth. Her bound hands which dangled uselessly from the ring in her collar tried futilely to protect her from his abuse of her mounds. Her hips shifted beneath him and her eyes had opened widely.

He lifted his head from her breast and grinned at her. "Enjoying our little fuck, Betty?" he asked tauntingly. "You have a wonderfully hot cunt. Give me a good squeeze, little birdie or I'll have you whipped."

Betty had lost herself in her reverie about her old college fuckbuddy and she realized that she was neglecting her duty to her master. She had been given lessons on how to tighten her fuck hole for its users' pleasure and she concentrated on the muscles there, giving the cock that possessed her a pleasure giving contraction. Her lusts were rising and she began to push her hips back up at the cruel man's feverishly. She wanted to get off desperately. It was the only thing that made her life bearable. She could feel her orgasm approaching, building higher and higher as the conscienceless cock grated across her pussy's inner lining. She squeezed it hard again and again, timing her contractions of her muscles with the cock's long, delicious outward motions. And then, suddenly, her body took over and her pussy began to throb and pulse of its own accord. "Ooooo! Ooooooo! Ooooooo!" she called out through her distended lips. Her mind was overwhelmed with pleasure. Her body shuddered and her thighs clamped against the strong, hard body between them. "Oh fuck me! Fuck me! Fuck me!" she yelled in her mind as the steel hard, thick rod continued to plough her depths.

Burnham exulted as he saw the birdwoman give herself over to her lust. His own passions rose and his cock began to jerk and spasm within her. "Ahhhhhh! Ahhhhhh!" he groaned as his fluids poured the length of his cock in hard, exciting pulses. "Ahhhhhhh! Ahhhhhhh!"

When his expenditures were exhausted, Burnham laid his body down over the still trembling slave. Her pussy was still giving him the benefit of its fading contractions as she gave out one last, well pleasured moan. He waited until she lay still, her body limp and relaxed beneath him and then he eased his softening meat from her womb.

"You are a good fuck, Betty," he told her as he stood erect and returned his cock to his pants. "Now get up before you leak all over my desk."

Slowly, the half bird, half woman came back to life. She was glad for the pleasure she had taken from the man, but shamed at his callous use of her. Burnham took her gag up from the desk and reinserted it inside her distended lips and then buckled it behind her head. When done, he patted her on the side of the face with his large, heavy, right hand.

"Since you seem to like fucking so much, Betty," he told her, "I'm going to send you down to the ponybarn. You know that almost all of the ponygirls are out in the pony camp with their drivers, and the trainers and stable boys are getting very horny with no ponies to fuck. I'll get one of the other slave girls to mind the desk for a week or two."

Betty shivered at her owner's command. She had seen how the men treated the ponygirls. They were cruel and used them callously, worse even than the Russian security guards. She didn't want to go there to be treated like an animal. She gave out a whine and tried to beg her lord and master with her eyes to pity her. But her effort had the opposite effect.

"Betty, you're not being a very good slave girl," Burnham told her, annoyed. He took a small pad of stickies on his desk and wrote on it. He tore off the sheet and placed it on her forehead. "Take this note down to the slavemaster before you go to the ponybarn. It tells him to give you twenty strokes with a cane. Hopefully, it'll teach you not to question my orders."

The former secretary's heart jumped into her throat at the thought of twenty blows from the cane. Her eyes began to tear and her body shivered. "Why have I been chosen for this cruel, hard life," she thought dismally. "Why? Why?"

Burnham saw that his birdwoman was overcome with unhappiness at the thought of her upcoming torture. She was really beginning to annoy him.

"Get going slut!" he commanded in a harsh, unforgiving voice. "If you're not down there in two minutes, I'll make it fifty!"

Betty gave a little leap of fright at her master's words and turned to flee. She had to lean over and bend her knees so that her captured hands could grasp the door knob and open the door. She gave out a low, dismal sob as she exited the room. She pulled the door shut behind her and ran down the stairs.

CHAPTER FIVE
MAUREEN

Irving and Maureen sat atop a small hillock overlooking the ponygirl camp watching the ponies being prepared for the upcoming race. It was a week and a half since Maureen had arrived at the Burnham estate. Irving was worried about her. She hadn't said a word since she arrived.

The day was slightly chilly, the feeling of fall was coming on quickly. But the sun was bright and there were only a few plump clouds drifting across the pale blue sky. Irving had brought along a little lunch for them, but Maureen had not eaten a bite.

The scientist had been surprised when he saw Maureen get off Burnham's private helicopter. The girl had been more than full figured when he had first met her, but now she had grown to almost gargantuan proportions. The thin, faded, yellow housedress she was wearing now that one of the cooks in the kitchen had found for her strained at its seams. Her flesh seemed to flow out of it all over. Her brown hair, which was just beginning to grow back in, was short and bristly. Whatever had happened to her after he had watched her being driven away from the Georgia farm house in an ambulance had obviously scarred her deeply. He had tried everything to bring her out of her funk. But the tall, heavyset, young girl just moped about the place following his suggestions docilely as if they were orders.

Maureen's mind was far away as she watched the fit, muscular former women down in the camp being harnessed for their carts. The races would start in about an hour, but every racing meet was preceded by a parade of the contestants for the delectation of the crowd. The camp site immediately below where she and Irving were sitting was occupied by the ponies that hauled the nine pony cabriolet, a large, ornate, gold trimmed carriage. One by one the tall, broad shouldered ponies were affixed between the traces.

It had been a great shock to Maureen when she had been taken from the premises of La Papaya, the Mexican whorehouse where she had served for many months. She had been treated cruelly there, fixed up to look like a pig and made to crawl around on all fours. The callous but creative madam there, Esmeralda, had been inspired to fix the morose, chunky, big boned slave girl up in porcine habiliments when one of her patrons had refused to consider her as a companion because she, "looked like a pig."

Esmeralda had forced the girl to spend her days on her hands and knees with her ankles tied up against the rear of her thighs and had pig ears and a pig nose glued onto her. She had even had devised a wiry pig tail that was implanted in the flesh of her rear, just above her anal opening. Her head and body were completely shaven. And she had her force fed vast quantities of high fat, high caloric foods to increase her already large bulk. The customers loved to make the pig girl squeal as they fucked her and Maureen was brought out for all the special parties.

But uniformed men had come and taken Maureen away. They brought her to a hospital in the isolated, southern Mexican city and left her there for almost two weeks. It had taken three days for the pretty, sympathetic nurses to soak off the pig nose and the pig ears. The tail had been surgically removed. And every day, the frightened, confused girl was made to walk, longer and farther each day, until she regained the full use of her legs.

Nobody bothered to tell Maureen that she was going to be taken away to this strange land where women were made to act like horses and naked, tattooed slave girls abounded. She had felt a moment of happiness when she saw Irving, but then it quickly faded. It was clear that she had been saved from the Mexican whorehouse through Irving's efforts, but when the brief surge of happiness had worn off, Maureen realized that she was now destined to be just another fat girl in a world of lithe, alluring, young women. At La Papaya, she had been fucked every day. The staff had seen to it that she was caressed to completion many times a day so that she would develop an addiction to physical pleasure. And she was the center of attention at the parties. She may have been a pig, but she was at long last the object of somebody's desire, no longer the homely, big boned girl who everybody shunned and who was laughed at and taunted.

But now, nobody fucked her, not even Irving. She saw the look in his eyes when she came into his company. He had saved her, but now he was saddled with her. And the other men gave her disdainful looks whenever she passed them. She had returned to her life as an outcast, an oddball, and she hated it.

"Come on, Maureen, why don't you have something to eat?" Irving asked her pleadingly. But Maureen didn't want anything to eat. She wanted to fade away, to die, if possible. When she had been a pig, she didn't have to worry about being a person. Everything was thrust upon her, she had no choices to make. She looked down at the strong, fit ponygirls. "Why can't I be like them?" she thought miserably. Anything would be better than being a fat, unhappy, ugly girl.

The scientist was at his wit's end. He couldn't go on like this. Now that he had saved Maureen, he felt like she was his responsibility and he was beginning to resent her for that. He decided to give consoling the girl another effort.

"I'm sorry for what happened to you, Maureen. I tried and tried to find out what Burnham did with you, but he wouldn't tell me. I know that you're unhappy. If there was anything I could do for you, I would do it. But I don't know what you want. There has to be something."

Maureen glanced at the small, well meaning man. She saw the sorrow in his face and the exasperation. What did she want? What did she want? She didn't know, other than to be relieved of the life of a reject, an object of derision and repulsion. She looked down at the pony camp. The last gorgeously shaped, lean, well toned ponygirl was being harnessed to the large carriage. The driver jumped up to the seat and took the reins in his two hands and gave them a yank while calling something out to the ponygirls in Russian. As one, they sprang forwards and, in a moment, the gaily decorated carriage was pulled away.

And then suddenly it hit her. What did she want? She knew what she wanted. More than anything she had ever wanted before. She turned to Irving and for the first time since she had been reduced to animal like status in the Mexican whorehouse, she spoke.

"I want to be a ponygirl," she said.

"What?" Irving responded, unsure if he had heard the young woman correctly.

"I want to be a ponygirl," Maureen replied in a low, matter of fact tone.

"You can't want that, Maureen. You can see how they're treated. It's horrible."

"No, I want to be a ponygirl. That's what I want."

Irving was astounded at the girl's request. Something had happened to her, he knew that, and now she was insane. That had to be the explanation.

"You can't just be a ponygirl for a little while, Maureen. Once you're a ponygirl, that's what you'll stay. I can't let that happen after all I've done to save you."

"Save me?" Maureen answered. She was surprised at her own audacity. But becoming a ponygirl had assumed a place as the most important thing in her life. "Look at me, Irving." Maureen demanded. "I'm fat and gross and ugly. Nobody wants to fuck me, not even you. I don't want to be an unhappy, fat girl any more. I want to be hard and muscled and fucked all the time. I want the men to stick their cocks in my mouth so I can suck them off and then whip me whenever they want. I want someone to pay attention to me. I don't want to have to think about what I am and when or how I'll ever be happy."

To hear such a determined stream of words from the woman's mouth was a shock to Irving. He had come to think of her as almost mentally retarded over the last ten days or so. He had wondered what had been going on in her fur covered head. He wanted to make her happy, to somehow relieve her agony from her terrible experiences over the last six or seven months. But not this! Not to become a ponygirl. And what kind of a ponygirl would she make. She would never be one of the sleek, fast ponies who pulled the fancy racing carts. She was just too big and broad shouldered. She would be an oddity among oddities, the subject of mirth and callousness. After all he had risked to save her, how could he let her succumb to this?

"I can't let you do it, Maureen, even if it could be done. It's just too terrible. It's against everything I believe."

"What do you mean you won't let me? You don't own me. And as far as your ethics are concerned, I see you looking at the pretty, little slave girls. I've seen you taking them into your room. What about that? And you never asked me once, not once!"

Maureen was crying now. This was just what she had been wanting to avoid. She didn't want human feelings any more. She wanted to be a thoughtless animal, trained to obey her masters. He had no right to tell her what she could or couldn't do. He had no idea what she had been through all of her life, always the ugly girl left sitting at the dances, the last girl picked for anything. Even the men who had bought the other girls who had been a captive with her in the underground prison where Irving and the other man had found her hadn't wanted her. When the horrible old man and woman who had kidnapped her had been killed and she could have been taken away for free, they had left her behind to die of starvation in her small, steel cell.

There was a long silence between the astounded man and the unhappy, distraught, young woman. In the background, they could hear the roar of the crowd at Burnham's racing track as the ponies were led in parade before the grandstand. Maureen's words had struck Irving cruelly. She was right. Who was he to tell her what she could or couldn't do? There was something in the air, it seemed, in Kalikastan, that changed you, a kind of virus that caused all sense of morality and ethics to slip from your mind. If he was to be honest to his pledge to the girl to give her what she wanted, he would have to help her, no matter how foolish or wrongful her decision seemed to him.

"Okay, Maureen," Irving said to the girl finally. "I'll see what I can do."

Late the next morning, Burnham had laughed heartily when he heard about Maureen's request. He was sitting behind his huge desk and Irving was sitting before him in one of the elegant Regency chairs. It had taken a lot of effort for Irving to broach the subject. He had castigated Burnham for his involvement in kidnapping women and enslaving them when he had first come to Kalikastan. And now look at him. Not only was he using the enslaved women to satisfy his growing lusts, but he was now proposing that the very woman he had demanded that Burnham save be dehumanized and made into a chattel.

"Ha, ha, ha, ha, ha!" Burnham laughed. "You've got to be kidding!"

"No, I'm not kidding, Mr. Burnham," Irving replied. "It's what she wants."

"Who wants a fat, dumpy ponygirl?" Burnham exclaimed. "She'd be a laughingstock!"

"Look, Mr. Burnham," Irving insisted. "I've done everything that you've wanted. The new racing cart is all finished and ready to go. It'll give you a big advantage in the fall tournament. It's the last thing that I'll ask for."

"Okay, Irving," Burnham answered, his face still reflecting his mirth. "But on one condition. I've got some more projects coming up where I'll need your assistance. You're going to stay here in Kalikastan and work for me. And I want you to get all the materials that you had prepared to send to the government and the papers back in the States. The blackmail is over, got it!"

Irving agreed. He waited in his chair disconsolately while Burnham made a telephone call to have his head trainer, Irkut, summoned to his office. It took about twenty minutes for him to arrive and he and Burnham just sat there silently while waiting. Burnham broke out in the occasional snicker and drank from a glass of scotch. There were two pretty, young women locked in the cages behind him and one kneeling on the floor by his desk. The one by the desk had long black hair that reached down below her shoulders to the middle of her back. She had sharp features and narrow, pale lips. Her hands were bound behind her and she was kneeling straight up with her legs spread and her back straight. Irving could not stop his eyes from wandering over her round, firm, pert breasts and her inviting, hairless nether lips. She wore Burnham's distinctive tattoo on her belly and her name, Alisha, tattooed across her chest. Her skin was very pale, almost wan, and her torso and limbs were thin.

The door finally opened and Irkut came in. He nodded to Irving and addressed Burnham.

"What can I do for you, boss," he said merrily. Irkut almost always had a pleasant demeanor to him. He was pleased that the chocolate ponygirl was doing well. She had won her race easily yesterday and was now on her way to the next meet, a four hour drive to the north. There was a yearling that had come in the other day and Irkut had spent the morning working her at the training ring. She was a dark haired, tall Chinese female, one of the benefits of Burnham's new deal with the Governor of the remote, westernmost province of that country: technology and dollars in, Chinese slave girls and cheap knock offs of Western goods out. She was clearly of peasant stock, thick, firm thighs and broad shoulders. It was only her third day and already he had her up to a long, intense sprint. Of course, you couldn't tell that she was Chinese from just looking at her, although her skin was dark and slightly yellowed. Her distinctive facial features were well hidden by her hood. But she was obedient and had serviced his cock readily, if somewhat inexpertly, with her widespread lips before he had placed her back in her stall in the ponygirl barn to spend some time resting and contemplating her new fate.

Burnham couldn't help smiling as he anticipated the ponygirl trainer's reaction to the news about Maureen. Everybody had seen her skulking about with Irving over the last week or so and the couple had been the subject of considerable mirth.

"I have a new ponygirl for you, Irkut," Burnham told him.

Irkut looked up, surprised. He was usually the first to know when a ponygirl van had arrived at the estate with a freshly dehumanized female. None had arrived today.

"Okay," Irkut replied. "When is it arriving?"

Burnham suppressed a giggle. "She's already here," he answered.

"Here?" Irkut asked. He looked at Irving and then back at his employer. "Where?"

Burnham turned to Irving. "Well, Irving," he asked, trying to mask a smile, "where is she?"

"She's out in the hall," Irving answered quietly. It was hard to believe that he was actually arranging for Maureen's enslavement. He shifted uncomfortably in his chair.

"Outside?" Irkut asked. "You mean the fat girl?"

Burnham could control himself no longer. He gave out a loud guffaw. "Y,yes, the fat girl," he managed to get out. "It seems that she wants to be a ponygirl."

Irkut looked back at Burnham with an incredulous look on his face. "She wants to become a ponygirl?" he said.

"That's what Irving tells me," Burnham replied. Smiling, he took a swig of his scotch and then put the glass back down.

The ponygirl trainer stood there lost in thought. Why would a woman want to become a ponygirl? Well, she was of the classic body type, tall, well built, if maybe just a little more so. She was just fat and homely. But the homely part didn't matter and he could probably thin her out in a few weeks. And then a thought occurred to him. One of the trainers had told him of a new ponygirl event that was being proposed for the Fall Tournement, a pilot project. It involved a strength and endurance race. This fat girl might be perfect. He bet she was as strong as an ox. All she needed was some training. But whatever her fantasy was as to what ponygirl life was like, she would not be prepared for the real thing.

Burnham looked at Irkut wondering what was going on in that inscrutable Russian mind of his. Was the man seriously considering it? Irving was looking too. The suspense was killing him. In a moment he was going to get up and call the whole thing off. It was ridiculous after all.

"Okay," Irkut said matter of factly. "I'll do it." At this he turned to Irving. "But you understand, once she's collared that's it. There's no going back."

"She knows that," Irving replied. "I told her."

"I don't give a fuck about her," Irkut spat out. "The moment she lets me put the collar on her, she can cry and whine all she likes. All she'll get for her efforts is the business end of a whip. It's you I'm worried about. You have to know that being made into a ponygirl is permanent. If you have any idea that you will be able to free her, even if she belongs to you, you better give it up. Don't come to me later saying you changed your mind. Anyone who tries to free a ponygirl commits a capital offense in Kalikastan. No exceptions."

Burnham took in this news and gave a little shudder. He covered up his discomfiture. "Let's make this clear, Irving. Once she's collared on my estate and she wears my insignia and disks, she's mine. I'll do anything I want with her. You can watch her run and train, but you'll have given up all interest in her. Finito. Got it?"

Irving nodded his head dolefully. "I understand," he said. "But you should make that clear to her. She's the one who wants it."

"All right, Irving," Burnham replied. "Bring her in."

Maureen had been sitting in the hallway quietly. She was wearing the same old housedress she had been wearing yesterday. Opposite her, sitting at the reception desk, was Burnham's secretary. The strange looking, gagged and tattooed woman kept staring at her as if she knew what was happening. Well, Maureen didn't care. She had made up her mind. Irving had insisted that she sleep on it and she had. She had thought about it all night. She knew that she was making the right decision. She didn't care how they treated her, as long as she didn't have to be human anymore.

The door to Burnham's office opened and Irving stuck out his head. "They want you to come inside," he told her. Maureen rose to her feet and shuffled over to the door and stepped into the room. She had seen the trainer come in while she was sitting outside. She looked at him questioningly. Was it yes or no?

"So you want to be a ponygirl?" Irkut asked her in his coarse, rough voice. "Is this true?"

Maureen looked at Irving who had sat back down in his armchair and then back at the trainer. "Yes," she said, her voice clear and resolute.

"Once you become a ponygirl, there's no going back, you understand that?"

"Yes," Maureen repeated.

"Take off your dress," Irkut commanded.

Maureen paused a moment. She had spent the better part of seven months naked. She had no shame about it now. But she was hesitant because of Irving. He had cared for her, tried to rescue her. In spite of what she had said to him the day before, he wasn't like the other men. But if she became a ponygirl, he would see her naked soon anyway. What did it matter, after all?

The heavyset girl lifted her dress by the waist and began to pull it over her head. In a moment, it was off of her and she tossed it aside. She wore nothing underneath. Her breasts were monumental, big and round and fluffy. Her belly, from months of forced eating, was bulbous and huge. Her thighs were heavy and so fat that when she put them together her feet stood a good foot and a half apart. But she was tall and had a broad back. Her skin was unscarred and smooth.

Irkut stepped up to the naked girl. "Put your hands on your head," he said rudely. When Maureen had complied, he took her breasts in his hands and began to massage them. They were bigger than his hands could take in all at once. He twisted and turned the fat nipples until the girl squirmed with pain. He crouched down in front of her and felt her thighs and shins. "Spread your legs," he told her curtly. Maureen moved her thighs apart. He slid his hands upwards and felt the insides of her thighs and then stroked her plump slit. Her hair had just started growing back and there was a covering of fuzz around it. His hand stroked and manipulated the soft flesh until her crevasse began to moisten and dilate. Her clit had become stiff and prominent and he petted and stroked it until the girl's body sagged and she gave out a little moan.

Satisfied, Irkut got up and stepped behind her, running his rough hands across her back and then down it to her round, full buttocks. He came around the front of her again and, grabbing her face with his hand, looked into her eyes. Irkut liked his women big and meaty. He was slender and a little under average height. There was something about a mass of female flesh surrounding him that pleased him. He released the girl's face and turned back to the room.

"Okay," he said. "She'll do."

Irving got up from his chair. "Maureen, are you sure you want to do this?" he asked, his voice tremulous.

"Don't talk to her," Irkut shot out. "Don't ever talk to her again. I don't want you anywhere near her. Forget her. In a little while, she won't even be a woman anymore. Understand?"

A dismal, unhappy look crossed Irving's face. He sat down in his chair dejectedly. "Okay," he answered meekly. "I understand."

Irkut went over to the wall and pulled a slave leash off of it. He circled it around Maureen's neck and clipped it to itself and then pulled it tight. Burnham had a cabinet in his office which contained the various impedimenta of female slavery in it and Irkut retrieved a shield gag and forced the business end into Maureen's mouth and then connected it behind her head. Without ado, he yanked on the leash and pulled the newly enslaved woman to the door.

Maureen followed the man obediently as he led her down the stairs of the mansion and outside. She had done it! She had really done it! A knot of fear began to build up in her belly. Had she made a mistake? Would she regret her decision? The man seemed cruel, crueler than the men who had had charge of her back at the whorehouse in Mexico. What would he do to her?

When they reached the ponygirl barn there were a few of the other trainers sitting around drinking vodka and killing time. There was not much else to do since the ponygirls were mostly all away. There were a couple still around, reserves for the larger teams and the yearling that Irkut was training. A few of the other men were fucking them now in their stalls. The men all looked up when they saw Irkut approaching, a large, fat, naked woman in tow.

"What's this, Irkut?" one of them asked merrily. "Is this your sister?"

Irkut didn't reply, but as he passed the man he struck him a blow in the face with his fist. It knocked him to the ground. Irkut turned to the other men. "Anyone else have any questions?" he snarled.

The men all looked at him sheepishly and then at the ground in front of them. Irkut wasn't the biggest of men, but he was among the meanest. Nobody wanted to fuck with an enraged Irkut.

The ponygirl trainer turned away from the men and brought his charge into the barn, shutting the door behind him. There were skylights on the roof of the barn and some elementary lighting, but without the light from the door, the interior was dim and it took a moment for his eyes to adjust. The frightened young woman stood before him, her hands still obediently on her head, her eyes looking at him dolefully. There was a glistening around the edges, the beginning of tears.

"I'll give her reason to cry in a minute," Irkut thought. "First I've got to get her all fixed up."

He stepped over to the equipment closet and retrieved a ponygirl collar and a black, stretchy neoprene hood and a pair of slave bracelets. He stepped behind the large, trembling woman and snapped the bracelets around her wrists. He pulled her arms back behind her. Her arms were too fat to allow the bracelets to be joined, but he had taken a small chain from the closet and he connected it to the two bracelets, confining the woman's hands behind her back. He took the leather covered, plastic ponygirl collar and snapped it around her neck. It was a tight fit. Standing behind her, he released the gag from her mouth and pulled the black hood over her head. It connected to tabs in the collar and shrouded the female's plump face. He took the gag and reinserted it into her mouth and connected the belt back behind her head.

Maureen whined when the gag was shoved home. She tried to look out of the little holes in the hood, but she could only see a tiny bit of the new reality around her. Her arms had already started to ache from their confinement. She could feel her body sweating from fear.

The girl had been barefoot when she had entered Burnham's office and now she needed to be accoutered in her black, shiny ponygirl boots. Irkut took hold of the ring in the front of the female's collar and pulled her to a bench along the wall. He pushed her down upon it so that she was lying on her back. He stepped away for a moment and returned with the largest pair of ponygirl boots that he could find. One by one, he shoved them onto her, buckling them tightly around her shins. He then pulled the new ponygirl back to her feet.

What had been, a few minutes ago, a young woman, was now a mere animal. The fact that her flesh was heavy and overabundant didn't matter. And neither did it matter that she had not yet been marked with the emblems of her new status. She was hooded and collared. Her face was permanently hidden away. He voice was irremediably taken from her. She wore the boots of her new profession and her hands had been made vestigial. She was now a creature to be molded into an instrument of her masters' wills. He would train her and she would bemoan her choice. But once Irkut took charge of a ponygirl, she would train well or die.

Maureen's head was tilted up by the front of her ponygirl collar. She couldn't see the cruel visage of her trainer, but she could feel his strength and determination as he stood in front of her. She had never been so frightened in her life. Her legs were shaking and her bladder released, sending a stream of yellow fluids down her thighs. She moaned in humiliation. But at the same time, she sensed that she had achieved a kind of liberation. Whatever this man did to her, whatever he made her do, she no longer had to worry about what people thought of her. She no longer had to pine about not fitting in, about being isolated and ignored. For a while at least, she would be the center of this man's attention. And as she grew stronger and fitter, the other men would pay heed to her as well. She was a ponygirl now and forever. She had left Maureen behind.

She was no more. As time went on, her life as a fat, ugly, young woman would fade into oblivion.

Irkut took hold of the heavy ponygirl's collar and brought her to the center of the open area of the barn. She shuffled over on her newly applied boots and gave out a mild whine from behind her gagged lips. A chain ran down from the ceiling and he hooked its end to the ring in front of her collar. He went to the wall and pulled it taut, until the rotund pony was balanced on the tips of her toes, her covered face pointed upwards. He went to the rack of whips on the wall and bulled out a long, heavy bull whip.

It was important for there be a clear, irrefutable demarcation in new ponies' minds between their former life as women and their new life as beasts. That was why their moment of dehumanization, traditionally thought of as the moment that they received their first real pony collar and hood, be dramatically emphasized. A good whipping served this purpose well. It also was an important harbinger of what their lives would be like from now on. They all tried to beg and plead for surcease, but the gags in their mouths suppressed all words. Thus, they learned that no amount of supplication would assuage their suffering. And they learned what true pain was like, for few, if any, of them had ever suffered the kind of physical torment a well applied whipping produced.

Normally, Irkut selected one of he milder whips for this part of a new pony's indoctrination. But this one had been walking around a few minutes ago a free woman. She had volunteered to become a ponygirl and she needed to have dispelled any notion that she would have any right to determine how she would be treated as soon as and as firmly and dramatically as possible.

Maureen heard the 'crack!' of the bullwhip as Irkut tested it in the air near her. She knew what it was and her body trembled in fright. Knowing that she would be whipped as a theoretical matter had been one thing. She had seen one of the men beat a ponygirl unmercifully not long after she had arrived here. And as a pig, she had suffered the lash many times. But this was somehow different. She danced on the tippy toes of her new ponygirl boots and began to moan in fear.

Irkut's first blow struck the heavyset pony atop her large, bulbous right breast. It made a loud 'crack!' as it landed and left a deep, red bruise. The sound of it striking the pony's flesh was followed immediately with a piteous, unrestrained howl from behind the pony's gagged lips. "Ooooooooooouuuuuuuuuu!" she screeched. "Ooooooouuuuuuuuu!" Her whole body jiggled like jello as she danced and hopped in place. Her body turned from him, twisting the long, heavy chain above her.

The second blow landed on the soft, pillowy and rotund left cheek of her ample ass. Another angry red mark arose immediately and the howling of the fat pony escalated. "Oooooooouuuuu! Ooooooooooou! Oooooooouuuuuu!" she called out. Her vocalizations of her excruciating sensations of pain were followed by what sounded like imprecations for surcease of her ordeal. "Ooooooooo! Eeeeeeeeee! Ahhhhhhhhhp! Eeeeeeeeeeee!" It was always the same. Irkut knew what she was trying to say. But it didn't matter.

The kissing of her breast by the cruel whip felt to Maureen like someone had thrust a knife into her. It was far beyond anything she had ever experienced. The pain exceeded her expectations a hundredfold. The second was as bad as the first. She didn't want to cry out and howl with pain. She didn't want to beg that the man, "Please, please stop!" But she couldn't help herself. Anyone would do the same. Even you.

Irkut took his time in delivering the strokes of the bull whip to the pony's squirming twisting body. He watched as the bright red marks accumulated over her breasts, her full, round belly, her oversized thighs. He struck her back and her arms and legs. Her howling continued to follow each moment of contact between her flesh and the hard, cruel leather, but she had stopped trying to form speech and just blubbered uncontrollably during the long, tortuous pauses. Having her head tilted upwards prevented her from knowing where any particular blow would land and Irkut walked around her quietly as she twisted and turned on her chain so as to surprise her. He followed no particular tempo, and a fierce, agonizing blow from the whip might be followed by another within a few seconds, or he might let her wait as long as a minute to suffer in anticipation of the next excruciating contact between flesh and leather.

When Irkut saw that the pony's body was marked sufficiently for his purposes, he decided that she had had enough. She would remember this time with him the rest of her ponygirl life. There would always be the time before her merciless whipping and the time after. Her memories would be divided between when she had no idea what torment could be delivered to her defenseless body and when she had gained that knowledge. Blood dripped from several of the harsh wounds and the pony's body was covered with rivulets of pink tinged sweat.

The satisfied ponygirl trainer stepped to the wall and lowered the chain from which the heavy, unhappy ponygirl dangled. She sank immediately to her knees. Her head was still held high by the chain that was connected to the front of her collar and Irkut stepped into her view. He could just see her black, dilated pupils behind the small, dime sized wholes. Her covered face was expressionless, but he knew that behind the hood her face was awash with tears and her lips down turned in an agonized grimace. He unhooked the chain from her collar and unfastened the shield gag from behind her head. It was time for the new ponygirl to service her master. He pulled the thick wad of leather from her mouth and, after removing his stiffened wand of flesh from his pants offered it to her mouth.

Maureen saw the demonic man ease his tool from his pants. Although besotted by tears, her body burning from the fierceness of her torture, she opened her lips readily to receive it. She was proud of herself. She had endured the man's abuse. She was aware of its significance as a right of passage and she welcomed it. She wanted to thank the man for her deliverance from self. Although it had been agonizing, far worse than she had ever anticipated, it was better than she had ever hoped.

With a thrill in her loins, Maureen subsumed the man's thick meat with her lips and began to suck on it readily. She reveled in its firmness and heat as she let her tongue swirl around its fat head. His groan of pleasure excited her and made her shudder with pleasure. She took her time, pressing her lips firmly against the shaft and dragging them down its length. He placed his hands on her covered head and guided her back and forth over his meat. When she felt the thick prick begin to pulse and throb in her mouth, she pressed her head hard down on the man's belly, taking all of his flesh within her, forcing the fat knob at its end into her throat.

Irkut moaned with unexpected ecstasy as the ponygirl serviced him. He had not anticipated the pony's enthusiasm or skill. As wave after of wave of pleasure shot through him, he congratulated himself on his acceptance of the challenge to train the giant female. At each spurt of his cock, he gave a little cry of pleasure.

When his load had been discharged, the wiry, experienced ponygirl trainer slowly eased his manhood from between the ponygirl's lips. He bent to the floor and picked up her discarded gag and pressed the long wad of leather home. When he had buckled it behind her head, he stepped back and snapped his fingers with one hand while motioning the pony upwards with his other. Slowly, awkwardly, the pony struggled to her feet. He would have to think of a good name for her, he thought. Her earnestness demanded something better than his first thoughts: Walrus or Hippo. Tomorrow, he would have her tattoos burned into her belly and on her chest. Her nether lips would be pierced and a large, brass ring run through her septum. The incipient growth of hair on her body would be shaven off except for a little tuft in the back of her head which would, eventually, grow into a long ponytail. No, the new pony deserved a name reflective of her spirit, something that would announce her strong character.

For now though, there was training to do. He needed to get her running around the training ring to start working off her excess flesh. When he was done with her, she would be a mountain of firm, solid muscle. And later, once he had her mounted in her stall, he would fuck her and make her available to the other men. She deserved no less.

The trainer affixed a leash to the ponygirl's collar and brought her to the door of the massive barn. Maureen watched him as he rolled it open, revealing the still bright, sunny afternoon. The glare of the sun and the way it made the day seem filled with color made Maureen swell with happiness. She felt the tug on her leash and stepped out of the barn and into her new life.

CHAPTER SIX
REWARDS

The two tall, well toned ponygirls had been strenuously running neck and neck for three quarters of the way around the track. Their svelte bodies were gleaming with sweat and their breasts bobbed and jerked beauteously on their torsos as they fought for primacy. The brightly colored, feathered plumes that adorned their heads danced above them and their long, loose ponytails dashed to and fro across their backs, recording each desperate stride of their taut, well muscled thighs. The dirt flew from the track where their shiny, black, ponygirl boots struck deeply into it. The traces which bound them to the small, streamlined carts behind them were taut and their diminutive and demonic drivers were lashing out with their fierce ponygirl whips and calling out their imprecations for speed, more speed! It was a classic contest between two well trained, frantically obedient beasts, but as they reached the far turn and began to enter the home stretch, the blue and gold hooded pony started to pull ahead.

The crowd was going wild. Ponygirl fans were well educated in the sport and the significance of the lead of the tall, big breasted, blue and gold hooded ponygirl was not lost on them. Even though there were still three racing meets left in the season, the ponygirl whose name they kept shouting in unison, "Molnya! Molnya!" would, with this victory, secure top seed in the fall tournament that would take place in about two weeks.

"Molyna! Molnya! Molnya!" they kept shouting as the pony took a two length lead on the yellow hooded one. By the time that it crossed the finish line, it was ahead by two and a half.

Anton Drabik lowered his binoculars and smiled. Lightning had done it again. He had put 10,000 kronskis on her nose. Not that there would be much of a payout. She had been the clear favorite at 3 to 5. But it was the principal of the thing. He always bet on her and not to now would threaten a jinx.

Drabik had other reasons to smile. His plan to unseat his lord and master, Axmail Grobgy was going well. The 4 million that he had liberated a few weeks ago had been spread around wisely and Drabik now awaited only the proper timing and the go ahead by the National Commission. Grobgy was a commission member and nobody knocked off a Commission member without the blessing of the Commission itself.

The journey from St. Petersburg to Mikhail's compound outside of Odessa, following his one man raid on Grobgy's warehouse, had been uneventful. The pretty blond whore had remained silent and obedient the entire trip. Before pulling out of the warehouse, he had bound her ankles together and tied them off to the springs under her seat. Her wrists had been joined in front of her and connected to her ankle ties so that her hands were held down below her waist. One of the men he had killed was apparently an exercise enthusiast and had a blue racquetball in his gym bag which was just the right size to stuff into the girl's mouth. It had puffed out her cheeks slightly and a little patch of blue peered out from behind her slightly distended lips, but it had the salutary effect of preventing her from speaking. The last thing that Drabik wanted after all the trouble he had taken to bring her along was to have to shoot her.

The drive was very long and for many miles the road was flat, straight and lonely. He had stopped at a little, isolated country store around five o'clock and bought a stick of dried sausage, a block of pungent cheese and a bottle of sweet, white, locally bottled wine. Before going in, he had rummaged through the blonde's pocketbook and taken out her identity card. Svetlana Oblenski was her name. She lived at 222 Leventov Prospect, Apartment 2b, or at least she had until now. He put it in his pocket and told the girl before he went in that he was going to mail it to some friends of his. If she escaped or called for help and got away, even if he was arrested, his friends would track her down and kill her and her entire family. With a small tear running down the side of her face, the girl nodded eagerly. She was waiting dutifully in the car when he emerged from the store.

He stopped about five miles later, pulling down a side road from the two lane highway and then down a little dirt road. When he came upon a small glade of trees, he pulled the car in behind them so that it could not be seen from the road. He was hungry and wanted to eat, but he also wanted to give the two sluts in the trunk the chance to pee. He didn't want them smelling up the trunk of his Mercedes.

Leaving the blond girl in the front seat, he opened the trunk and let the other girls out one by one so they could squat in the grass and relieve themselves. They gypsy girl gave him a hateful glare when she emerged, but the brown haired girl was obsequious and obedient. Their panties were still bunched up around their knees and Drabik removed them so that the girls could relieve themselves.

Before each one climbed back into their little traveling prison, he double checked the tape on their mouths and their bindings. The gypsy girl had managed to work her taped mouth free and after giving her two harsh slaps across her face for disobedience, he took two lengths from the duct tape that he kept in the trunk for such emergencies and doubled it up over her mouth.

When the other girls had been reinstalled in the trunk, Drabik released Svetlana and let her take her turn squatting in the foot high, yellow and pale green grass. She looked up at him gratefully as she released her pent up water in a strong, yellow stream. The sun was just setting over the tops of the trees and a soft light, tinged with red hues, filtered through them. He spread a blanket out that he had in his back seat over the grass and brought the blond girl over to sit on it with him.

Drabik had freed her bound ankles and the tie that connected her wrists to them. She knelt expectantly in front of him while he lay on his side and used his knife to cut off pieces of the spicy, hard sausage and chunks of cheese. The girl watched him dolefully as he ate and washed down his meal with the golden, fruity wine. Her pretty, pale cheeks bulged out slightly due to the presence of the small, blue racquetball in her mouth. Taking his time, enjoying his primitive repast among the isolated, bucolic setting, Drabik relished the vision of the delightful, short haired, lanky whore. His cock stirred as he recalled the assiduousness with which she had sucked him off a few hours ago. He was satisfied that he had made the right choice in bringing her along.

Wanting to see more of the girl's comely body, Drabik instructed her to place her bound hands behind her head and to spread her legs wide until the short, brown leather skirt that she wore rode high on her thighs exposing her delightful, straw covered slit. The girl's pert breasts pushed against her blouse. He leaned forwards and unbuttoned it, pushing the sides of the blouse apart so that her female attributes could be clearly seen. Her nipples were hardened with fear and little goose bumps ran the circumference of her wide, dark areolas. Satisfied at his view of the girl's now brazenly presented, desirable body, Drabik leaned back and continued his impromptu meal.

As he masticated his cheese and sausage, he idly flicked the end of his finely honed knife at the tips of the girl's breasts, teasing them until he saw a trickle of sweat roll down from her neck between her firm mounds. So far, he was glad of his decision not to waste her. As he took another swig of the fruity, golden yellow wine, he debated whether to give her something to eat. But he decided that her fear might cause her to regurgitate any food that she consumed. And anyway, he wasn't here to serve her pleasures, it was the other way around.

When the sausage and cheese were gone, together with about half of the long necked bottle of wine, Drabik shoved the cork back in the bottle. The vision of the blond girl's delectable body in combination with the alcohol had given him a hard on and he decided that he would give vent to his lust before he started back on the road. He shucked off his heavy boots and drew off his pants and shirt. The girl watched him attentively and he caught a little whine from her when his thick, hard cock came into view. It was the only sound she had made since the warehouse in St. Petersberg.

Drabik took hold of the girl's slender, round shoulders and guided her to her back. She placed her bound hands above her head on the soft, brown and red checked blanket. He lay down next to her and ran his heavy, scarred hand over her flat, smooth belly. "Svetlana, Svetlana," he thought, "you are a pretty wench." As he stroked her soft skin, he felt the girl's body tense. "Relax, whore," he told her, his voice gruff and demanding, staring callously into her soft, blue, frightened eyes. "What's one more cock up that slutty pussy of yours? Eh?" He said. He slid his hand down between her pale, slender thighs and seized the mound of her sex. She gave out a little moan as he imprisoned her cunt in his hand and her long, beautiful body shuddered. Her pubic hair was soft and sparse and her labia were thick and hard. "Loosen up, my little whore," Drabik said softly but menacingly. "If you don't give me a real good fuck, I might change my mind about taking you with me. It would take months for anyone to find your body here. I'm taking a big risk with you riding in the front seat with me and I want to make sure that it's worth it. Understand?"

The girl's eyes widened as Drabik's unveiled threat. Her distended lips began to tremble and a tear ran down the corner of her sparkly, blue, right eye. She nodded fervently and spread her long, graceful legs wider and raised her knees to give the killer better access to her sex. She closed her eyes and pushed her hips up so that her pussy could meet the man's caresses. Drabik noticed a small drop of blood near her left nipple, the result of a pinprick from his razor sharp knife. He leaned over and licked it off, dragging his rough tongue over the hard, distended button and then subsuming it with his lips.

As Drabik suckled at the girl's small, round, hard breast, he felt her body begin to lose its rigidity and her pussy began to soften. He probed between her nether lips with the tip of his finger and found her incipient moisture there. He sucked hard on the tasty nipple in his mouth until he heard the girl give out a low moan of pleasure. He lifted his head and seized her other delectable mound and pushed his fingers deeper into her lubricating cleft. She began to rock her hips gently, in a tantalizing, rotating motion, letting his fingers fuck her. Drabik began to toy with the little nub at her sex's apex and he felt the girl's body tremble beneath him.

"This whore's practically a trained slave girl already," Drabik thought. His chest lay across her belly as he lapped at her nipple, alternating flicking it with his tongue and sucking hard on it with his lips. The heat of her body was enflaming him. Her leather skirt was pushed up around her waist and her silken, yellow blouse lay open on either side of her. Abandoning the girl's now loose and sex ready cunt, Drabik caressed the soft insides of her widespread thighs and then let his hand drift north, along her tight, pleasurable belly, over her breasts and then up to her graceful, pleasing face. He placed his fingers between her thin, taut lips and eased the racquetball out of her mouth, replacing it with his tongue.

Having decided, in a bid to ensure her own survival, to facilitate her own rape, the girl's tongue met his eagerly. She kissed him back hard, circling her bound hands over his head and down to the back of his neck, pulling him into her. She moaned as she kissed him and her body squirmed enticingly. Seeing that the girl's lusts were fully engaged, Drabik threw his legs between hers and pushed his knees up against her soft thighs until her legs were spread wide on either side of his hips. He could feel the soft skin of her inner thighs along his sides. Eager for coitus, Drabik took his cock in his hand and guided it to her plush, soft, lower entrance. Its fat head spread her now enflamed lower lips and was welcomed by her hot, moist inner flesh. Drabik groaned with pleasure as his hard tube of meat slowly sank within her. The girl gave out a long, languorous sigh and pulled his lips harder against hers.

"She's a good whore all right," Drabik thought through his lust filled haze. He grabbed her hands from around his neck and pushed them to the ground above her. Breaking the contact between their lips, Drabik raised his head and gazed at the girl's impassioned face as he stroked his cock long and slow along her hot canal. Her lips were parted and her breath was coming heavy. Her hands were balled into tiny fists and her head was thrust back, exposing her long, smooth neck. She met each thrust of his hips eagerly, clamping down on his thick meat with the walls of her pussy each time he delved deep within her.

Drabik wanted to see her come before he released his load into her. He began to increase the tempo of his thrusts, rasping the top of his cock along her hardened clit each time he pushed inside her. She began to make a faint mewing sound as her climax approached. Her eyes had opened and she was staring back at him intently. Suddenly her eyelids began to flicker and her body shuddered. "Ohhhhhhhhhhh!" she moaned feverishly. "Ohhhhhhhhh! Ohhhhhhhhhhh!" Her thighs clamped against him tightly and her pussy began to convulse with pleasure. Her dainty nostrils were flaring and her eyes had rolled back. Her face was a picture of ecstasy. "Ohhhhhhhhh! Ohhhhhhhhhh!" she yelled now, "Oh! Oh! Oh! Oh!" as each intense contraction sent another message of electrified pleasure to her body.

Drabik felt his own orgasm rise from his aching, needy balls to his well pleasured shaft. He groaned deeply and felt his cock begin to throb and spasm. His body tensed and he pounded his hips into the girl's as his climax overwhelmed him. "Grrrrrrrahhhhhhhhh!" he yelled out. "Auuuuuuuuugh! Auugghhhh!"

As his cock's throbs faded, Drabik took hold of the girl's short, bright yellow hair and thrust his tongue back in her mouth. The warm pleasure of her tongue accentuated the fading spasms of his cock. When they finally subsided, he let his body fall heavily against the girl's while his breath returned to normal and his beating heart slowed. The girl's chest rose and fell as she too recovered from her climax. Her thighs relaxed their grip on his hips and her knees fell to her sides. Drabik raised his head and peered into the girl's face. "Nicely done, whore," he told her. "I guess I'll let you ride along a little longer. Now open those pretty lips of yours again."

When the girl's pale pink lips slowly, but obediently, parted, Drabik returned the small blue racquetball to her mouth. A look of intense unhappiness spread across her face.

It was starting to get dark and he wanted to be on his way. He rose from the girl's body, letting his now flaccid cock slide free of her slippery canal. In a few moments he had dressed and he rebuttoned the girl's blouse while she knelt cooperatively on the blanket, looking at him dolefully. He put her back into the passenger seat, retied her ankles and connected her bound wrists to them. He folded the blanket and returned it to the back seat of the car together with the half empty bottle of wine. It was another two hours to Mikhail's. He got into the driver's seat, roared the engine back to life and headed back to the highway.

Mikhail was delighted with the three women Drabik had delivered, not to mention the suitcase full of heroin. Drabik had been right about the popularity of the tiny, child like, big breasted, brown haired girl. Mikhail's men had a little party with her that evening. Mikhail chose the gypsy girl for himself. Drabik spent the night with the blond girl and it proved to be as rewarding as he had anticipated.

Also, as he had anticipated, Grobgy had been going mad trying to contact him. When he returned his master's calls, Drabik feigned shock and surprise at the news of the raids on Grobgy's outposts and agreed to arrange immediate reprisals at the gangs who Grobgy suspected as complicit. On Grobgy's orders and using Mikhail's compound as a base, he knocked off two of the Bronski brothers' places and one of Kerensky's. It was just what Drabik had wanted. Grobgy was acting outside all of the rules and the National Commission would be just that more conducive to Drabik's bid to supplant the aging gangster. And it had added a sizable amount of money to Drabik's war chest.

The blond girl, Svetlana, had cried when Drabik left to return to Kalikastan. He had handed over her leash to Mikhail and given her a little pat on the head in appreciation of her week's worth of delectable services. She had not spoken a single word to him in the time that she had been his prisoner, but as he turned to go, she made a muffled plea to him through her gag. She was kneeling naked at Mikhail's feet, her hands locked behind her. Mikhail was a rotund, black bearded fellow, amiable enough in appearance, but a cruel and callous slaver underneath.

"Oh, don't worry about her," he told Drabik, laughing. "The Greek is coming by next week and I'm sure we'll find her a good home." He pulled her leash up, raising the unhappy, svelte, blond girl's head high. "I'm afraid that you've spoiled her. I'll give her a nice long session with the whip this afternoon to improve her manners."

Drabik looked at the beautiful body of the unfortunate girl. She was trembling and her eyes transmitted her misery at her fate. It was too bad that he couldn't take her with him. But not only did she know too much, it would violate the general ban in Kalikastan against enslaving Slavic girls for use there.

"Just make sure you're ready when I give you the word," Drabik returned. "You have the list of men that have to be taken care of. Everybody has to be hit at the same time. I'll be taking care of things in Kalikastan."

Mikhail had been chafing at limitations that Grobgy had placed on his operations for a long while. He stood to gain a much bigger piece of the pie once Drabik took over. But he would need careful looking after. A man who was prepared to betray his employer once might do it again. Once he had consolidated his power, it might be smart to replace Mikhail with one of his army friends.

Now, back in Kalikastan, looking over the emptying grandstands, the losers finding their way to the exits, the winners lining up merrily at the betting booths, Drabik felt a sense of power and destiny infuse him. All this would soon be his, including the delightful ponygirl that he had just watched scrambling to victory.

* * * * * * * * * * * * * *

Lightning pulled her cart along the narrow dirt track that wound its way among the ponygirl encampment. She wore a ring of fresh, colorful flowers around her neck, the symbol of her victory. It had been, despite all appearances, a close run thing. The other pony had been fast. Very fast. But her driver's greater experience had saved the day. She had literally run the other pony into the ground, starting out at full speed and going wire to wire at maximum effort. Only her greater reserves had proved the difference between failure and success, something that her driver had built up in her.

The happy, sweaty pony had sensed that she had achieved something special by the way that the crowd had reacted. No one had told her that she was competing for first seed in the fall tournament, she didn't even know that she had qualified, wasn't even sure that there would be another tournament after this round of racing meets. No one told a ponygirl anything. All she did was run when she was commanded, fuck when she was compelled to. She had often overheard the men talking, but her knowledge of the strange language that they spoke was rudimentary at best. She had guessed from its sounds that it was Russian, but she wasn't really sure and there was no one she could ask. She had no idea where she was. Maybe it was Russia, maybe it wasn't. She barely knew any of the other ponygirls' names, the two inch high, blue, Cyrillic writing on their upper chests being mostly indecipherable to her. She had heard her driver called 'Jerzy' by the other men. She had heard the cruel, diminutive man call out to his slave girl, the skinny, frail, abject black haired girl who cared for her, as Natasha. That was about all she knew.

But there had been more than the usual exuberance in the winner's circle after her race. She stood there, exhausted and naked, her chest still heaving from her exertions. Her owner, the huge, black bearded man, had been there and he was smiling ear to ear and laughing. He had petted and suckled at her breasts to the glee of the happy, surrounding crowd. When the garland of pleasantly smelling flowers had been draped over her neck, there had been an enthusiastic round of applause. She had even seen her driver smiling and joking with the other men and women, a rare sight indeed.

The only dark moment was when she had seen the icy face of the woman who she knew as her trainer's girlfriend. She had stared at her with her evil eyes, a promise of pain and hurt in them. Lightning didn't know her trainer's name, but she knew of his obsession with her, an obsession that was reciprocated. Being separated from him during the racing season was the hardest thing of all to bear. The misuse and cruelty of her driver was a mere annoyance compared to her longing for the tall, dark eyed, scar faced man who had first taught her what it meant to be a ponygirl. Despite the horrors that he had visited on her, despite the whippings and beatings he had inflicted, she craved his attentions, lived for the times that he deigned to possess her with his thick, relentless, pleasure giving cock.

The price of her attraction for the hard, brutal ponygirl trainer was the enmity of the young, beautiful, black haired woman. Once, she had whipped her to an inch of her life and Lightning knew that only her value to her owner, who apparently stood in some relation to the woman, prevented her from visiting more torment. A chill ran through her veins when she caught the black haired woman staring at her, but it had passed as she received the caresses and pats of the other people around her and the woman faded into the crowd.

As she passed through the ponygirl camp, towing her cart, her driver on board behind her, the men from the other encampments called out their congratulations to him, waving their caps and raising their glasses as she trotted by. When she reached their encampment, Jerzy hopped down off of the sulky cart and commanded the black haired slave girl to release Lightning from her traces.

Using her ring in her collar, and after removing and setting aside the tall, feathery blue plume that had adorned her head during the race, the thin, wiry, black haired girl pulled the tall and expectant ponygirl to the center of the wide, grassy circle. Its limits were denoted by four foot high cloth panels colored with wide blue and gold stripes. Natasha knew from the roar of the home crowd and the wreath around Lightning's neck that she had won her race and what the win significated. The pony had earned her pleasure and would get a round fucking as a reward. Natasha didn't really begrudge the pony her infrequent pleasures, but fucking was a zero sum game as far as their dwarfish master was concerned and what he gave to the pony he could not give to her. Natasha had been his slave for three years now and she had handled a number of ponygirls for him. She bore her own scars from where he had whipped her. She hated and despised him. She had not experienced a kind word or a soft caress from him since he had taken her from the whorehouse where he had purchased her down in the capital. But, nonetheless, like the ponygirl, fucking was one of the few pleasures that she could experience and she looked forwards to the use of her owner's thick, hard cock. But tonight, his attentions would be devoted primarily to Lightning.

Natasha guided the tall, strong ponygirl to her knees. Lightning stood a good foot taller than her, was broader of shoulder and much stronger. But she acceded compliantly to the wraithlike girl's commands. Natasha had beaten Lightning many times for disobedience, real or imagined. One word from the naked, black haired girl and a world of abuse would be visited upon her by her driver, ever eager to prove his mastery over her. So Lightning, even though she detested being handled by the skinny, black haired slave girl, obeyed her every command as if it were the word of her master.

Jerzy tossed aside the blue and gold silk cap that he wore on racing day. His slave girl had prepared a bottle of vodka and a small glass for him on a little table near the door to the camper and he threw back a fiery, celebratory shot. First seed in the tournament was no small thing. He would be able to rest Lightning as she defeated the ponies from the bottom of the list easily in her first few races, saving her strength for the more difficult heats. He poured himself another shot and downed it quickly. He turned towards the center of the small encampment. He had a ponygirl to service.

Lightning was expectantly on her knees, her thighs spread widely, her large, sweaty breasts presented brazenly. He reached for them and caressed them with his small, but powerful hands. He could see the dark centers of the pony's pupils peering out from behind the tiny holes for her eyes, the only real sign that there was a former human creature behind the tightly fitted blue and gold hood. Gripping the pony's thick, stiff nipples in his fingers, he pinched and turned them until the pony gave out a whine of pain and pleasure. The leather covered, steel bit spread her lips cruelly and the sound of her dismay combined with anticipation of her use emerged from behind it. Jerzy reached around back behind the pony's head and loosened the straps that held the bit in place and then removed it from the pony's mouth. Before she received her pleasure, she would have to pay obeisance to his.

Jerzy lowered his zipper to his pants and drew his hardening instrument from inside. He placed his hands on the pony's shoulders and made her lower her head until her mouth was level with his cock. Her lips were parted obediently, but she had learned the hard way not to anticipate her master's commands.

To be able to take possession of her driver's cock was a significant event in the ponygirl's life. On days when she did not race, and on the few racing days when she did not succeed, Lightning would kneel despondently before her master, her lips open, while he pleasured himself in front of her, using her mouth only as a receptacle for his spunk as it jetted out from his thick cock. Later, after he had beaten her, she would kneel in her cage and watch while the diminutive driver pleasured the black haired girl. Or at night, after she had been put to bed on the ground under the camper that was the driver and his slave girl's home, she would listen as the man drove the slave girl to repeated pleasure above her. Her body would squirm with her own need as she listened to the girl's moans and screams of blissful ecstasy.

But today, the day of a victory, Lightning would enjoy the full benefits of her master's thick, heavy meat, and having it between her hungry, impassioned lips was just the start.

Lightning waited patiently until Jerzy gave her the sign that she could take possession of his manhood with her mouth. She happily moved her head forward, relishing the sensation of the thick, ribbed meat as it passed over her lips. She moaned with satisfaction as she clamped her mouth around it and let her tongue dance across its bulbous head. She relished the salty, hot taste of the man's flesh as she pushed her head down towards his belly and took the length of his steel hard pole inside her.

The naked and sweaty ponygirl took her time, enjoying her reward. Her eyes were closed within the confines of her hood, and all of her consciousness was focused on her task. She could feel her breasts as they swayed and jerked beneath her chest each time that she drew her head back and forth, dragging her tightened lips across the length of the rock hard cock. Her bound hands twisted and tugged at her bindings behind her unconsciously, not unlike the wagging of a dog's tail, not functional to her task, but evidence of her delight in performing it.

When Lightning felt her master take a firm grip on her long, chestnut colored ponytail and begin to urge her head up and down on his cock faster and harder, she knew that he reward for her efforts would not be long in coming. She heard the man's familiar moan and sensed his body tightening as his cock flowed relentlessly along her tongue and lips. He gave out a sharp cry and the meaty weapon within her mouth began to throb and spurt. It was this that she missed, the feel of a discharging cock within her mouth, the transfer of its power and passion to her. The ponygirl moaned and received each jet of her master's cum with relish. She sucked and licked at his member assiduously until the throbs faded beyond detection and his orgasm had died.

When Lightning opened her eyes, her master's cock slipping from between her lips, she noticed that some of the other drivers and grooms had entered their little camping area. They slapped the smaller man on his back in congratulations on his orgasm and began to laugh and joke with him. Lightning was not disconcerted at having been seen pleasuring her master's hard cock. In fact, quite the opposite. She knelt back proudly on her haunches, knowing that her master would be pleased that she had demonstrated her devotion to him in front of his confreres.

There was little time for the ponygirl to linger. Jerzy took a seat in his little chair by the camper door and Natasha, after inserting a thick, leather gag into the pony's mouth and buckling it behind her head, took hold of the ring in her collar and urged her to her feet. Lightning had worked hard today and her strained muscles in her legs and back needed attention. It was customary for Natasha to give Lightning a rubdown as soon as possible after her race was complete and the rest of her reward for her victory would have to wait.

The black haired slave girl led Lightning over to the workout table on the side of the encampment area. It was tilted and Natasha leaned Lightning's back against it and then let it slide forward so that the pony was lying flat on her back. Her booted ankles were raised and spread wide and locked into place. The slave girl turned behind her and retrieved a bottle of the soothing, muscle relaxing lotion that was applied to Lightning's skin after every workout. She spread a large dollop in her hands and proceeded to use her small, but strong hands to stroke down the length of Lightning's firm, well muscled thighs and shins.

The pony girl's view was of the bright blue sky above her as the knowledgeable and expert hands massaged her legs' tender muscles. The girl's hands had a definite, firm rhythm to them and very quickly Lightning's body began to soften and glow in response. Natasha seemed to know just how to bring maximum pleasure to the pony's valuable, well trained muscles and sinews. Lightning moaned as the hands sent wave after wave of delicious sensation to her brain. She felt the hand of the slave girl dip between her stretched out thighs and find the soft, hairless lips of her sex. While one hand stroked and caressed her taut belly and her full, plump breasts, the other hand worked its way along the tender sex lips and over the her bud of pleasure until the engorging lips began to spread and her cleft began to lubricate with desire.

It had been three days since the last race and the last opportunity for the ponygirl to feel the pleasure of her sex in the throes of orgasm. Oftentimes, the slave girl would tease her into a frenzied, impassioned state, only to leave her to burn, her needs denied. Jerzy would have whipped the black haired slave girl severely if he knew that she let the pony come without permission. But today, Lightning would be permitted to achieve the completion of her lusts. Today, she had won her race.

The chestnut tailed pony's hips writhed and churned on the table as the slave girl's hands drove her further and further along in her need. The hand that had been caressing her now moist and dilated crevasse left it and Lightning could feel the small, tender hands of her master's servant draw slowly and lightly over the inner skin of her thighs. She felt the long, black hair of the slave girl lay across her belly as she lowered her head to her loins. And then she felt the hardened tip of the slave girl's agile, experienced tongue delve between her excited love lips and trace a long, languorous line between them.

Lightning moaned with pleasure as the slave girl's tongue danced along her fevered slit, probing deep into her steaming canal and then playing over the stiff clit at its apex. The slave girl's teeth seized the distended button and bit down on it just sharply enough to send a message of pleasure mixed with exquisite pain through the ponygirl's loins and then along the channels and synapses of her nervous system and into her already overwhelmed mind. The ponygirl arched her back and spread her imprisoned thighs even wider as she luxuriated in the pleasure brought by the slave girl's mouth. She moaned and her body shook as the girl's thick tongue lapped again and again the length of her slit, pushing itself deeply into her moist, hot pussy and ending with a caress of her quivering clit.

Lightning knew that her master and the other men who had gathered in the encampment space were watching her demonstration of carnal delight, but she did not care. Their eyes did not burn into her body like the eyes of the 'normal' people, the spectators, did. These were men, if not inured, at least acclimated to the vision of naked, former women in the throes of passion. Although the sight of her writhing and moaning body would undoubtedly be a source of inflammation to their lusts, it was not a source of novelty to them. Lightning need feel no shame before them since her sexual excitement was expected, in fact demanded. And she knew that, sooner or later, once the ponygirl racing season was over, they would recall her sexually enticing form, her lascivious display of passion, and take their own pleasure with her time and time again.

Natasha let her tongue play repeatedly over the hardened nub atop the pony's fevered loins. The ponygirl's strong, sleek body stiffened and she gave out a long, deep moan from behind her gagged lips. Her hips began to press her loins against Natasha's mouth and her mighty thighs quivered. Natasha gripped the pony's thighs firmly with her arms as she kept her lips and tongue held firmly against the pony's throbbing quim. She was coming, hard and long, and Natasha rode her expertly, driving her well past the point of pleasurable endurance. "Mmmmmmmm! Mmmmmmmmmm! Mmmmmmmmmmmmmmmm!" the pony called out through its gag as its orgasm overwhelmed her. "Mmmmmmmmmmm! Mmmmmmmmmmmmmmmm!"

After a full minute of gut wrenching, body thrilling convulsions of her sex, Natasha finally allowed the ponygirl's pussy to come to rest. Her own pussy glowed with need as the aroma of the pony's discharge filled her senses. She could only hope that her master would have something left for her at the end of the night, or that, perhaps, he would lend her out to one of the other drivers or grooms. But he would do neither if she did not complete her tasks satisfactorily, and her massage of the ponygirl was only half done.

Lightning lay mesmerized by the afterglow of her climax as she felt the slave girl's hands release her widespread ankles from the table. She knew the routine and she passively allowed the girl to roll her to her belly on the long, thin, padded, exercise board. The slave girl released first one hand, and then the other from behind her back, and affixed them to rings at the top of the board. Lightning allowed the girl to manipulate her arms without struggle. She had closed the flaps to her hood before doing so and even though her hands were no longer behind her,

Lightning had no view of them. It had been many months since she had seen her own hands. The ponygirl tried to visualize them as the slave girl started to work the soothing, muscle relaxing liniment into her back and the back of her thighs. She wiggled her fingers and opened and closed her fists as if in an effort to ensure that they were still a part of her.

Women had hands, not ponies. It might have been easier if her masters had removed them entirely. But such disfigurement of a pony was considered unaesthetic. Part of the mystique of ponygirls was their approximation of the human, female form, the knowledge that what had once been a free, independent woman had been transformed into an obedient, sexual beast. And so the ponies' arms and hands were allowed to remain, vestigial evidence of their former existence, a kind of talisman of their masters' power over them.

Lightning's brief reminder of her former humanity passed as the strong, skillful hands of the black haired slave girl pressed into her extended back and shoulder muscles. The rhythm of her caresses soon had Lightning's mind floating into a world of dreamy pleasure. Her body, already soothed and comforted by the oral delight the slave girl had given her, seemed to melt on the platform as the girl worked her muscles thoroughly. Her hands massaged the muscles of her buttocks and along her thighs and down to the well sculpted, firm tendons behind her shins, and then back up to her long, strong, broad back and the muscles of her shoulders. Lightning moaned softly as she allowed the sensations to take her far, far away from her captivity, into a languorous zone of contentment. Ponygirls took their pleasure where they could find it.

When Natasha had completed her ministrations to the ponygirl's flesh, she returned her hands behind her back and locked her wrists into the long, thick strap that descended from the back of her ponygirl collar. Lightning was dazed and almost stupefied by the slave girl's attentions, but she responded immediately, automatically, when she felt the tug on her collar indicating that she should rise. The table tilted back up and she was brought to a standing position, her thick, black ponygirl boots finding purchase in the soft, grassy earth.

Natasha left the ponygirl's eye flaps down as she pulled her back to the center of the small encampment. Lightning could sense the accumulation of a small crowd of drivers and their male assistants and she could hear them laughing and joking with each other in their deep, gruff voices. Obediently, she followed the directions of her master's slave and she sank first down to her knees and then bent over, her forehead pressed to the soft, cool grass.

Lightning spread her thighs widely in anticipation of the administration of her reward from her driver. Her heavy, full breasts pressed against her knees. She was facing away from the small semi-circle of men and she knew that her hairless mons and the well used, diminutive circle that guarded the entrance to her bowels was presented ludely to them. She knew that the gap between her smooth, shaved nether lips was moist and ready for her master's penetration and that the men could almost certainly note the glistening of her needy crevasse. But she did not care. There was only one thing that she cared about now, only one thing that she wanted, the caress of her driver's thick hard meat inside her.

Jerzy was enjoying the companionship of his fellow drivers. They were a close fraternity. A couple of the drivers from the other team had come over and were congratulating him on his strong win. The driver of the other 3000 meter sulky, the one he had defeated, was there too and he saluted his better with a large tumbler of vodka.

The dwarfish driver let the ponygirl kneel expectantly for his cock. Admiring her taut, plump haunches and her well presented sex, he thought of the tournament to come. Another trophy would look good on the mantelpiece in his mansion down in the capital where he spent his winters. He may be small and he may be deformed as other men saw it, his short but muscular arms, his large man sized head atop his tiny frame, his child like size. But he was a master of his craft, the driver of ponygirl champions, and no one could take that away from him. In the winner's circle, he stood as tall as anyone else.

After his fourth of fifth shot of vodka, Jerzy decided that it was time to give the ponygirl her reward. He stood up from his tiny chair and pulled his racing blouse up over his head and tossed it aside. The other men gave out a cheer as they saw that he was preparing to give the kneeling, naked ponygirl a taste of his cock. They gave another collective shout as he stripped off his boots and then the shiny, blue and gold, silken racing pants and dropped them into the grass. His thick cock, long and fat, was already hardening in anticipation of its insertion into the ponygirl's flesh. He gave it a little tug as he stepped up to her, coaxing it the rest of the way into stiffness.

Lightning had been patiently awaiting her master's attentions. She had taken her mind to that place where she blocked out all of the cruelty and hardness of her existence, something she had learned during the many hours that she had stood bound and gagged in her stall in the ponygirl barn affixed to the rail across the front of her waist, her legs spread and anchored to the floor awaiting her masters' desires. Her wrists rested against her back, one below the other and her hands were closed into little fists. When she sensed her driver approaching, she spread her knees wider and raised her hips, positioning herself for his penetration.

Jerzy ran his small but strong hands over the smooth, round globes of the pony's rear and then down along the outsides of her thighs. His cock was protruding outwards like a sword and he allowed it to rest along the crack of her ass as he let himself enjoy the smoothness and hardness of the pony's flesh. He felt her body quiver in expectancy as he handled her. He had driven many a ponygirl, had ridden to victory many times behind them, but this was one of the best. There may have been faster ponygirls he had driven, stronger ones too. But this pony had heart, a need to win that surpassed all of the others.

He had had his doubts when Grobgy had insisted that she run the 3000 meter race this season. It was unusual enough that she had championed at the 1500 as a yearling. But he had been right. And the 3000 meter was the pinnacle of the sport and no pony had ever won the 1500 and the 3000 meter championship in consecutive spring and fall tournaments. He would be making history and he knew that his accomplishment would be the subject of admiration in the circles of ponygirl racing aficionados for years to come. And who knew what she might accomplish next year or the year after that. Sulky ponies tended to peak after three or four seasons, and Lightning would not be a champion forever, but her records would be etched onto the walls of clubhouses across the small nation along with pictures of her, naked and hooded, standing in the championship circle with him at her side.

The ponygirl driver's lust began to get the better of him and he stirred himself from his reveries. He reached down between the ponygirl's outstretched thighs and caressed her hairless nether lips, delving his short, stubby fingers along her moistened cleft. The men behind him were yelling out catcalls of ribald encouragement as he positioned his hips behind the pony and pressed the fat helmet of his rigid meat between her distended love lips.

Lightning moaned as she felt the tick cock enter her. She shuddered with pleasure as it slowly began to fill her, spreading her hairless and tingling love lips apart and scouring the walls of her hot, needy cleft. The thick meat dragged along her stiffened pleasure bud sending a wave of ecstasy through her. She kept her forehead pressed firmly into the grass in front of her and clamped her teeth down on the thick, leather intruder that filled her mouth. Her driver's hands had a firm grip on her hips as he sank his manhood slowly and deeply within her. She groaned with pleasure, wanting it all inside her. When she felt her master's hips press snugly against the backs of her thighs, she moaned again.

The small but powerful man gave the pony long, languorous strokes with his cock. He was in no hurry and the ponygirl deserved his full and patient attentions. Her pussy was hot and tight as he glided slowly back and forth, letting its warmth send wave after wave of pleasure to his body. It did not take long for the pony to come. Her body shook and her moans grew frantic as her pussy began to throb and convulse around his cock. Although the sensations of the climaxing pony drove his passions higher and higher, he did not let it influence the slow, steady, firm strokes e was administering to her. His head was thrown back and his eyes closed to slits as he enjoyed every second of his immersion in her flesh.

When her pussy began to give out its hard, pleasurable contractions, Lightning thought that she would go mad. Her whole body shivered and shook as the pleasure coursed through her. Her mind was focused on the abrasion of the little man's fat cock along her cunt's fevered walls. There was nothing else in the entire world. The shouts and laughs of the other men had faded away. All thoughts of who she was and what she had become disappeared. There was only the pleasure shooting through her and the certainty of its continuance as her first climax began to fade and she began to build to another.

Jerzy maintained his steady stroking of the pony's sex as her second orgasm shot through her. Her pussy gripped his meat hard on each contraction of its muscles. He was coming closer and closer to his own point of no return. When the pulsing of her pussy ebbed, he quickly withdrew himself from her sopping, distended crevasse and pointed his prick at the smaller target above it. His hands pressed on the pony's hips, lowering them to facilitate his goal and he ruthlessly pushed his fat cock inside the dainty hole. His fever was on him now and he began to thrust his cock along the sensitive, tender opening to the pony's bowels at a frenzied pace. The combination of the tight grip of her delicate ring around his cock and the murky heat of her bowels made his knees weak. When his thick pole began to jerk and throb within her, he gave out a mighty groan and began to pump harder and harder into her.

The delirious pony thrilled at the penetration of her rear by the impassioned man. She had been taught to take pleasure at this portal and the rasping of the thick cock along the sensitive ring of flesh triggered another hard, intense orgasm. She bit down hard on the thick leather between her teeth and called out her pleasure in a loud, mighty moan. She could feel the dwarf's man sized cock explode within her and the warmth of his discharge spread itself in her bowels. Her hands were gripped tightly into fists and her body convulsed as she received her pleasure.

The satisfied dwarf gave Lightning's buttocks a fierce, appreciative slap as he withdrew his now flaccid meet from her tiny aperture. His slave girl was waiting with a wet and soapy towel and he washed himself with it before rejoining his fellows for a final toast. Tomorrow was a travel day and he would be going to bed early in anticipation of an early rise. The slave girl had brought out his regular clothes while he had been fucking the ponygirl and he drew on his jeans and work shirt before saying good night to the other drivers.

The feed wagon arrived shortly afterwards. It was pulled by two of Grobgy's work ponies and driven by one of the stable hands. In the back was a brown haired, naked slave girl who jumped down and produced his covered platter of steak and potatoes. He took it from her and sat down at his little chair and table and began his meal.

Natasha brought over to the wagon two large, brown, porcelain bowls and the brown haired girl scooped ladlefuls of a thick, nutritional gruel from a large vat. As the wagon pulled away, Natasha placed one of the bowls on the ground before the still kneeling ponygirl and opened her eyelets and removed her gag so that she could feed. She took her own bowl over to a spot next to her master and, sitting on the ground cross legged, began to consume her fare.

It was customary to feed the slave girls who helped service the ponygirls the same food as the former human females received. It was a tasteless mush, but carefully prepared to satisfy the nutritional needs of the females. Slave girls may have retained their humanity, barely, but there was no sense wasting any effort to supply them with gustatory delight. Natasha did have two advantages over the ponygirl, however. One was that occasionally her master would feed her a bite of his own meal, a piece of steak or pork, depending on what had been prepared, and maybe a lump of potato. The other was that, since she had the full use of her hands, she could eat her mush with a spoon.

Lighting eased herself forward and dipped her head into the large bowl. Careful not to soil her hood, she lapped up the thick porridge-like substance greedily. Her body was still tingling from her bout of fucking, but she knew that if she did not conclude her meal before the slave girl was done that it would be taken away. And then she would be beaten for not finishing it.

The sun had fallen below the horizon and Natasha had lit the kerosene fueled lamps that circled the encampment. Lightning knelt still dutifully while the slave girl and her driver packed away most of their gear into the back of the camper. When she was done, the slave girl urged her to her feet and snapped a leash onto her collar. It was time for her trip to the latrine.

The ponygirl encampment was a flurry of activity as all of the drivers and their slave girls prepared for the next day's trip. Natasha led Lightning down the hard dirt pathway that wound its way through the encampment. Other ponygirls were taking the same trek and Lightning could see through the tiny eyelets of her hood a parade of tall, buxom, well built ponygirls being led by obedient, naked slave girls along the pathway. There was a short line at the latrine and Lightning and Natasha patiently waited their turns. Normally, no one cared where a ponygirl pissed or shat, but the concentration of a large number of the racing animals in such a small space mandated that their evacuations be made in a sanitary manner.

Natasha wiped and cleaned Lightning's privates thoroughly when she was done and led her back to their camping area. Jerzy was sitting in his little chair smoking his pipe when they returned and he ordered Natasha to bed the ponygirl down for the night. Lighting knelt while the slave girl brushed her teeth and then replaced her thick leather gag. Following the slave girl's lead, the ponygirl crawled beneath the camper and lay on her back on the thin pallet that served as her bed while Natasha removed her heavy, black, ponygirl boots. Her ankles and thighs were bound together with thick leather straps and then affixed to posts that had been pounded into the ground. Small chains were attached to the sides of her collar and fastened to posts on either side of her head. It had been getting rather chilly at night and the slave girl drew a thick, heavy blanket over the ponygirl's body and tucked it in around her in a cocoon-like covering. When she was satisfied that the ponygirl was properly secured, she closed the tabs over the eyelets on her hood and crawled back out from under the camper.

Lightning was tired from the day's exertions and relaxed from her sexual congress with her driver. But the time between when she was locked in place for the night, whether in the encampment or in the ponygirl barn, and when sleep claimed her was the time of day that she rued the most. Her vision was totally obscured and her body was locked into immobility. Try as she might, she could not but be reminded of what she had become and what she had lost. She had no idea how many nights she had spent as a ponygirl. They seemed endless. She had been a person once and she often thought of her prior life while she waited for unconsciousness.

For some reason tonight her remembrances were especially strong. Her mind went back to her little apartment she had back in Tennessee, her job at the tavern in Grafton, the joking and kidding she had often received from the men, rednecks mostly, who had frequented it. She had had a boyfriend too who she had broken up with just before she had been kidnapped. She missed him, missed everything about her prior life. She gave a little moan as the pain of her recollections ran through her. "Maddy. My name was Maddy then," she thought. Would she ever be free again? She doubted it. The men who had turned her into an animal were too coldly efficient to allow her ever to escape. And where would she go? She didn't even know where she was. No one but her cruel captors did.

Lightning could hear the winding up activity of her driver and his slave girl. She tried to concentrate on the sounds to bring herself out of her dismal memories. She was a ponygirl now and would never be anything else, she was sure of it. Even as she felt her eyes filling with tears, she tried to regain her acceptance of her state. Soon, she was certain, the racing season would end and she would be returned to the ponygirl barn. She would see her trainer again, the hard, scar faced man who had molded her into what she now was. She longed to be possessed by him again, to feel his need for her. Her flesh yearned for him.

She brought a vision of his impassioned face into her mind and was comforted by it. Slowly, as her troubled mind calmed, she felt her body relax into drowsiness. In a few moments she was asleep.

End of Book Seven.